Mr Pink-Whistle Stories

'Are you the bad boy that burst Susie's balloon?' asked Pink-Whistle in a deep voice just near to Big Jim's ear. The boy nearly jumped out of his skin.

'Oooooh!' he said in fright, looking all round. But of course, he could see no one at all.

'Did you hear what I SAID?' boomed Pink-Whistle. 'I said, "Are you the bad boy that burst Susie's balloon?"'

'I-I-I-did burst a b-b-b-b-balloon,' stammered Big Jim in a fright. 'It was an accident.'

'That's not the TRUTH!' said Pink-Whistle angrily. 'You did it on purpose.'

'Who are you?' asked Big Jim. 'And where are you? I can't see anybody. I'm frightened.'

Other Enid Blyton titles available in Beaver

Mr Pink-Whistle Stories

Enid Blyton

Illustrated by Rene Cloke

Beaver Books

A Beaver Book
Published by Arrow Books Limited
62–65 Chandos Place, London WC2N 4NW
A division of Century Hutchinson Limited
London Melbourne Sydney Auckland
Johannesburg and agencies throughout
the world

First published in 1941
Revised edition published in 1969 by
Dean and Son Limited
Beaver edition 1981
Reprinted 1984, 1987 and 1988
© Copyright Enid Blyton 1941
© Copyright Darrell Waters Limited 1969

Enid Blyton is the Registered Trade Mark
of Darrell Waters Limited

Set in Times
Printed and bound in Great Britain by
Cox & Wyman Ltd, Reading

ISBN 0 09 954200 5

1. The Adventures of Mr Pink-Whistle

Contents

1

The little secret man

'It isn't fair,' shouted Mr Pink-Whistle, 'it isn't fair!'

He stamped round the room in a rage, and his big black cat looked at him in alarm, and put her tail under her, out of his way.

'Here I've just been reading about a poor man who saved up and bought a nice new teapot for his wife – and on his way home a boy on roller-skates banged into him and broke his precious teapot!'

Mr Pink-Whistle put his hands under the back of his coat, pursed up his lips, and looked at his cat. 'Now is that fair, Sooty?' he shouted. 'Is that fair? Did anybody buy him another teapot? No! And look here – here's a picture of a little girl who ran to pick up something for a friend, and was knocked over by a motor-car! Now, I ask you, Sooty – is *that* fair?'

'No-ee-oh-ee-ow,' answered Sooty in surprise.

'Well, I don't think it's fair either!' said Mr Pink-Whistle. 'I do think that if people are kind, they should be rewarded, not punished – and what's more, Sooty, I'm going to do something about it.'

'Oh-ee-ow!' said Sooty, waving her tail a little.

'Sooty, you know that I'm rather a lonely little man, don't you?' said Mr Pink-Whistle with a sigh; and he stroked his big black cat, who began to purr at once.

'You see, Sooty, I'm not like ordinary people,' went on the little man, sinking down into a chair. 'I haven't any real friends except you. The reason is that I'm half a brownie and half a proper person – so the brownies don't like me much, and ordinary people are afraid of me because I've got brownie ears and green eyes like you.'

'R-r-r-r-r-r-r,' purred Sooty softly. She knew how kind her master was, even if he was only a half-and-half.

'*But,* Sooty, I've got a secret!' whispered Mr

Pink-Whistle into his black cat's pointed ear. 'Yes, I've got a secret that I've never used yet. I can make myself invisible whenever I like!'

Sooty didn't know what Mr Pink-Whistle meant. She stared at him out of eyes as green as her master's.

'I'll show you what I mean, Sooty!' said Mr Pink-Whistle. He shut his eyes and murmured a few strange words that made Sooty tremble and shiver.

And then Mr Pink-Whistle disappeared! One moment he was there – and the next he was gone. Sooty blinked her eyes and looked all round the little warm kitchen.

Her green eyes nearly fell out of her head in surprise. Where, oh, where had Mr Pink-Whistle gone?

Sooty heard a faint giggle – and there was Mr Pink-Whistle back again! Sooty put her ears back and looked alarmed. 'Mee-ow-ee-ow!' she said. She hoped her master wasn't going to do this sort of thing very often.

'Now, that's my secret,' said Mr Pink-Whistle, pleased. 'And what I'm going to do, Sooty-cat, is to go into the big town and look out for unlucky people. I shall go into their houses, and I shall disappear into thin air, so that they don't know I'm there. And I shall see that they get a reward for being kind! What do you think of that for a good idea, Sooty?'

'Wow-ee-ow,' answered Sooty.

'You'll stay here and keep house for me,'

said Mr Pink-Whistle, 'and I'll come back and see you often. Now I'll pack my bag and go. I won't let unfair things happen to people. I won't! I won't! I may be only a half-and-half, but I'll just show the world what I can do!'

He packed his bag, rubbed his face against Sooty's soft head, ran out of the front door, and waved good-bye.

Sooty watched her kind, funny little master go, and wondered what he would do.

'He won't be happy away from his cosy little home,' said Sooty. 'I know he won't. I wonder whose house he will go to?'

Now, in the nearest town lived a hard-working little woman called Mrs Spink. She had four small children, and it was very hard to feed and dress them properly. They didn't have many treats, but they were good little things and didn't grumble.

One day they all came rushing home from

school in excitement. There was Teddy, with blue eyes and golden hair; there was Eliza, with red curls; there was Harry, with golden curls; and there was Bonny, with a mop of dark hair like a sweep's brush. They tore into the kitchen and made Mrs Spink jump so much that she almost upset the pan.

'Mother! Mother! There's a party at school on Thursday and we're all to go!' cried Teddy.

'But you haven't got any nice clothes,' said Mrs Spink. 'Not any at all! You've only got the ones you have on.'

'Can't you wash them, Mother, and make them nice and clean?' asked Eliza, almost in tears at the thought of not going to the party. Why, they had never been to one before!

'Well, on Wednesday afternoon you must all go to bed, so that I can wash your clothes ready for the party the next day,' said their mother. 'That is the best I can do for you.'

Teddy, Eliza, Harry, and Bonny were quite willing to spend an afternoon in bed if only their mother would get their clothes ready for the party. Then she could wash them, iron them, and mend them.

So on Wednesday afternoon all the four children undressed, got into their ragged little night-clothes, and cuddled into bed, with books to read. Mrs Spink took the dirty clothes into the garden, set up her wash-tub, and began to wash all the clothes — socks, stockings, vests, knickers, shorts, shirts, petticoats, dresses, jerseys — goodness, what a lot of things there were!

Mrs Spink sang as she worked. She saw a funny little man with big ears and curious green eyes looking at her over the fence as she rubbed and scrubbed.

'Good-day,' he said; 'you sound happy!'

'Well, my four children are going to their first party tomorrow,' said Mrs Spink, squeezing the dirty water from a frock, 'and that's enough to make any mother happy! Poor little things, they don't have many treats. I'm just washing the only clothes they have, so that they can go clean and neat.'

When she looked up again, the funny little man was gone. That was strange, thought Mrs

Spink. She hadn't seen him go! She pegged up all the clothes on the line, emptied her tub, and went indoors to get the tea.

And do you know, the line broke, and down went all the clean clothes into the mud! Would you believe it!

Poor Mrs Spink! When she came out to see how the clothes were getting on, she could have cried. All of them were far dirtier than before!

'Well, well!' said Mrs Spink, in as cheerful a voice as she could manage. 'I'll just have to wash them all again, that's all!'

So she set to work once more, and put all the clothes into her wash-tub again. How she rubbed and scrubbed away! She didn't see the funny little green-eyed man again – but he was there, all the same, watching her. He was sitting on the fence, quite invisible.

'It isn't fair!' he muttered to himself. 'After she washed all those clothes so beautifully! No, it isn't fair!'

Mrs Spink couldn't mend the line. It was so rotten that she was afraid it might break again, so she took all the clean clothes and spread them out flat on the grass at the front of the house to dry. Dresses, petticoats, socks – they were all there, as clean as could be.

Mrs Spink went in to take the kettle off the fire, for she really felt she could do with a cup of tea. Mr Pink-Whistle slipped in behind her, though she didn't see him. He sat on a chair,

and thought what a nice, clean little kitchen it was.

And then a dreadful thing happened. Two dogs came into the front garden, and what must they do but run all over those nice clean clothes! They didn't miss a single one! So when poor little Mrs Spink went out to get them, there they were all covered with dirty, muddy foot-marks.

She didn't cry. She just stood and looked and gave a heavy sigh. But Mr Pink-Whistle cried! The tears rolled down his cheeks, because he was so sorry for Mrs Spink.

'It isn't fair!' he whispered to himself. 'She worked so hard – and it was all for her children. It just isn't fair!'

Mrs Spink gathered up all the clothes and put them into her wash-tub again. She washed them clean for the third time, and she hung them up on the big airer that swung from the kitchen ceiling. Then she went upstairs to see how the children were getting on.

'I'll have to iron your clothes in the

morning,' she told them. 'First, the line fell down and then two dogs ran over the washing. It's all in the kitchen now. Nothing can happen to it there.'

But she was wrong. Something did! A big heap of soot tumbled down the chimney, and when Mr Pink-Whistle looked up at the clothes they were all black with the flying soot!

'How dare you!' cried Mr Pink-Whistle, shaking his fist at the soot. 'How dare you! Oh, I can't bear this! I can't. I must put it right; I must – I must!'

And out he rushed to put things right – funny old Pink-Whistle!

2

Mr Pink-Whistle puts things right

Well, what do you think Mr Pink-Whistle meant to do? He meant to go and buy new clothes for all the four children! Good old Mr Pink-Whistle!

He was so upset to think that the clothes had been spoilt for the third time, after Mrs Spink had worked so hard and so cheerfully, that he had to blow his nose hard to keep from crying.

'It's not fair!' he kept saying. 'Why do these things happen when people try so hard? I won't have it! I shall put it right. It's no good being sorry about things if you don't do something to put them right!'

He quite forgot that he was invisible still, and that people couldn't see him. So, when he walked into a draper's shop and the door-bell rang, the girl there was most alarmed to hear a voice and to see nobody!

'I want to see some party-clothes,' said Mr Pink-Whistle. 'For two little boys and two little girls.'

'Oooh!' said the shop-girl, frightened, for she could still see nobody. 'There's somebody speaking and there's nobody here! Help! Help!'

'Oh, sorry!' said Mr Pink-Whistle, remembering that he couldn't be seen. At once he came back again, and his fat little body, big ears, and green eyes appeared in front of the surprised girl.

'Now don't run away or do anything silly,' said Mr Pink-Whistle. 'It's a secret I have – I can make myself disappear or not. Please show me the children's clothes you have.'

The girl looked into Mr Pink-Whistle's kind red face, and knew that he couldn't harm anyone. She took down some boxes and drew open some drawers. In a little while she and Mr Pink-Whistle were talking about what would be best for Teddy, Eliza, Harry, and Bonny to wear at the school party.

They chose new vests, warm and white. They chose knickers and socks, two pretty petticoats, two pairs of grey flannel shorts for the boys, and two blue silk frocks for the girls. Mr Pink-Whistle chose a green jersey for Harry and a red one for Teddy.

'Would that be all, do you think?' asked the girl, who was really quite enjoying herself now, for Mr Pink-Whistle had told her all about poor Mrs Spink, and she was feeling quite excited to think of the surprise that this funny little secret man was planning.

'Well – what about hair-ribbons for the two girls to match their frocks?' asked Mr Pink-Whistle. 'Or don't girls wear them now?'

'Oh, of course they do!' said the shop-girl, and she measured and cut two fine hair-ribbons of blue silk for Eliza and Bonny. 'Oh, and have the children shoes, sir? Did those get spoilt too?'

'Well, Mrs Spink didn't wash the shoes,'

said Mr Pink-Whistle. 'But I remember seeing them in the kitchen – very poor old shoes, too. I'd better have four pairs, I think.'

So they chose brown shoes that they thought would fit the children – and then that was really all. The girl did everything up in a big parcel and gave it to Mr Pink-Whistle. They beamed at one another, pleased to think of the secret they both shared.

Mr Pink-Whistle paid for the things. Then he said good-bye and went. He ran straight back to Mrs Spink's. He nearly forgot to make himself disappear, but just remembered in time. Then he opened the door and marched in, unseen by anyone.

Mrs Spink was still upstairs with her children. She didn't know anything about the sooty clothes downstairs yet. Mr Pink-Whistle looked round the black kitchen and frowned.

'I can't put the children's clothes here,' he thought. 'They would get sooty. What about the next room?'

Now in the next room was a big chest of drawers where Mrs Spink kept all the clothes of the family, and all the sheets and towels. Mr Pink-Whistle tiptoed to it and pulled the drawers open. The top one and the bottom one were empty. So Mr Pink-Whistle carefully and neatly put the boys' clothes into the top drawer and the girls' clothes into the bottom one. They looked lovely. Mr Pink-Whistle felt very happy as he packed them in.

Mrs Spink ran down the stairs to the kitchen. When she saw the sooty clothes and the black kitchen, she gave a cry of horror. And then, because she was so tired, she sat down on a sooty chair and began to weep.

'My beautiful washing!' she wept. 'Oh, I did think nothing more would happen to it! I'm too tired to do it again – but what will the poor children say if they've no clean clothes to wear at the party tomorrow? Oh dear! Oh dear! Things are very hard!'

The children came running down the stairs to see what was the matter with their mother. Mr Pink-Whistle watched them from the other room. Would they be angry? Would they be sulky – or very, very sad?

When they saw what had happened they were full of dismay and horror, for they knew that their poor mother had already washed the clothes three times. They flung their arms around her and hugged her.

'You won't be able to go to the party, my dears!' wept their mother. 'I'm too tired to wash the clothes again.'

'Mother, *we* don't mind!' cried Teddy.

'Mother, it doesn't matter a bit!' cried Eliza.

'Don't you cry, Mother; we'll help you wash again tomorrow,' promised little Bonny.

'We don't mind about the party!' cried Harry, though he did really mind, dreadfully.

'Nice children, kind children!' said tender-hearted Mr Pink-Whistle to himself, feeling for his handkerchief again. 'Oh, I'm glad I'm here to do something! I can't bear things like this to happen!'

'You're the best children in the world!' said their mother, and kissed them all. 'And that's just why you, of all children, should have a treat. It isn't fair!'

'No, it's not!' said Mr Pink-Whistle in a loud whisper. The children heard it, and looked surprised. Mr Pink-Whistle thought it was time that they saw what he had done for them, and he pulled open the top drawer and rattled it a little.

'What's that noise?' said Mrs Spink in surprise. 'I hope the cat isn't in my parlour, messing things up!'

They all went into the little parlour. They didn't see Mr Pink-Whistle of course, because

22

he was invisible, but they bumped into him without knowing it!

'Who has opened this top drawer?' wondered Mrs Spink, catching sight of the half-opened drawer. She went to shut it – and then she stared – and stared – and stared!

'Look!' she said in amazement, and pulled out of the drawer all the new socks, jerseys, vests and shorts belonging to the boys. 'New clothes! And new shoes too! Good gracious! Where did they come from!'

The girls pulled open the other drawers and soon found their new clothes in the bottom drawer. How they squealed and shrieked when they saw their blue frocks and ribbons to match!

In a trice the four children dressed themselves. Mr Pink-Whistle had guessed their sizes exactly. They all looked as sweet as could be, and if Mr Pink-Whistle had been their father he couldn't have felt prouder of them all.

'I don't understand it, I don't understand it!' said Mrs Spink, thinking she must be in a lovely dream.

'Now don't be frightened,' said Mr Pink-Whistle suddenly, 'because I'm going to *appear*. One, two, three – and here I am!'

And there he was! All five looked at him in astonishment. 'Did *you* put those new clothes there?' asked Mrs Spink.

'Yes, I did,' said Mr Pink-Whistle. 'I'm tired of seeing and hearing and reading about things

going wrong in this world. I can't bear it! It's not fair! So I'm just taking a little holiday to put some of the things right. And I was so upset about your having to wash those clothes so often that I felt I *must* go and buy some new ones. I do hope you don't mind.'

'You're a darling!' cried Bonny, and she suddenly hugged him. It was the first time Mr Pink-Whistle had ever been hugged and he thought it was lovely.

'Well, this is my first try at putting things right,' he said. 'I'm glad it is a success. Now be sure you enjoy your party tomorrow, my dears!'

'We couldn't help enjoying it, with all these

fine clothes!' cried Eliza, dancing round the room in her blue silk. 'Thank you, dear kind little man!'

Mr Pink-Whistle felt so happy that he thought he would burst. He hurriedly muttered the magic words that made him invisible again, and he disappeared. 'Good-bye!' he cried. 'Good-bye! I'll come and see you again sometime. I'm off to find something else to put right. Good-bye!'

'Good-bye!' cried the children, wondering where their queer, green-eyed friend had gone. He was off through the falling night, as happy as could be.

'Now for something else!' he said, with a skip and a jump. 'Now for something else!'

And he'll find it all right, as you'll very soon see!

3

The girl with the broken doll

Well, Mr Pink-Whistle's next adventure was with a little girl who had a beautiful new doll. Her name was Jessie, and one day when she passed by the toy-shop window, she saw the most lovely baby-doll she had ever seen, sitting there looking at her.

The doll was dressed in woolly clothes, and had a round woollen hat on its head with a bobble at the top. Its eyes were wide open and had long lashes. Its mouth smiled, and it had tiny little shining nails on its fingers and toes.

Jessie stood still and looked at the doll for a very long time. She loved it with all her heart. She longed to have it in her arms to hold. She longed to put it to bed in her toy cot.

'How much is that doll, Mummy?' she asked.

'It is very expensive,' said her mother, looking at the ticket on it. 'It is eight shillings and sixpence. Don't ask me to buy it for you, because I haven't even got two shillings to spare!'

'No, I won't ask you, Mummy,' said Jessie. She turned away from the doll, and went home. But all the time she was having tea she

remembered the doll's face and how its big brown eyes had looked at her, with their long curling lashes. And when she was in bed that night she remembered the doll again and wished she had it with her to cuddle.

'I shall save up, and save up, and save up till I have eight shillings and sixpence,' said Jessie to herself. 'Mummy says if you want a thing badly enough you can get it in the end, somehow! So I will get that lovely doll. Its name shall be Rosemary Ann. Sometimes I shall call her Rosemary and sometimes I shall call her Ann!'

Then Jessie began to save up. She saved all her Saturday pennies. She saved two shillings and sixpence that she had for her birthday. She saved a shilling that Uncle Fred gave her and a sixpence that Aunt Flo gave her. Every time

Mummy gave her a penny for running an errand or helping, she put that into her money-box too. She didn't spend anything on sweets.

She found a little sixpence in the street one day, and as she couldn't find out who had lost it, Mummy let her put that in her money-box too. And at last, after three whole months, she had eight shillings and sixpence!

'This is the most exciting day of my life,' said Jessie to her mother that morning. 'I am going to buy that new doll for my very own. She is to be called Rosemary Ann. She has such a lovely face, Mummy, and you should just see her dear little finger-nails and toe-nails!'

Jessie got the cot ready for her new doll. She found a doll's cup and saucer for her to drink from. She got ready her doll's pram to fetch Rosemary Ann from the shop. Then she put her eight shillings and sixpence into her bag and set off happily, thinking joyfully of the lovely doll that would so soon be hers.

There it was, still sitting in the window. Jessie ran inside the door, put down her money, and bought the doll. And at that very moment Mr Pink-Whistle came along, looking for an adventure! He couldn't be seen, for he was quite invisible. He wouldn't let himself be seen in the town if he could help it, because people laughed at his big ears and green eyes.

He saw Jessie's happy face and was pleased. He followed her into the shop without anyone

knowing. He saw the little girl buy her doll. He watched her take it into her arms and hold it there lovingly.

'You feel beautiful,' said Jessie to the doll. 'Your name is Rosemary Ann. I saved up for you for three whole months. I didn't buy any sweets. I didn't spend even a ha'penny, because I wanted you so badly. And now, you darling Rosemary, I've got you! You're mine! There's a cosy cot waiting for you at home, and a chair, and a cup and saucer – and there's your pram outside ready to take you home!'

The doll looked up at Jessie out of her big eyes. Jessie pulled the woolly hat straight and hugged Rosemary.

'I'm happier than I've ever been in my life!' she said. Mr Pink-Whistle beamed all over his red face. This was what he liked to hear. So many people were sad or hurt or disappointed, but now here was someone happy. He followed Jessie out of the shop and watched her tuck the doll up carefully into the blue pram. Then Jessie took the handle and began to push the pram proudly home, hoping that people would look into it and see the fine new doll.

But almost at once a dreadful thing happened. A crowd of boys came along with a big dog. They were shouting and laughing, and the dog was very excited. It kept jumping all around the boys and trying to lick their faces.

And just as the boys and the dog reached Jessie, the dog jumped up to one of the boys, fell sideways, and knocked Jessie's little blue pram right over!

Rosemary Ann was jerked out on to her head. There was a loud crack, and Jessie gave a scream.

'Rosemary! Oh, Rosemary's broken!' The little girl picked up her poor doll, and looked in horror at the broken face. The nose was smashed, and the lovely eyes had gone inside Rosemary's china head. She was quite, quite spoilt.

'I say! I'm sorry our dog did that!' said one of the boys. 'It was quite an accident. Shall we whip the dog?'

'Oh no,' said poor Jessie, with hot tears trickling down her cheeks. 'Don't whip him. He didn't mean to do it. Oh, I'm so unhappy.

I've only just this minute bought Rosemary Ann, and I saved up for three whole months to buy her. And now she's broken, the poor, poor thing!'

'Perhaps your mother will buy you another one,' said a boy.

'I shan't ask her to,' said Jessie, wiping her eyes. 'She hasn't got much money.'

The boys ran off with their dog and soon forgot about Jessie. Mr Pink-Whistle was left, standing invisible beside the pram. He was terribly upset. He sniffed so loudly that Jessie heard him and looked around. But she couldn't see anyone, of course.

Mr Pink-Whistle felt angry and upset and sad and unhappy all at once. He walked round the corner and stamped up and down in a rage. 'It isn't fair! It isn't fair! That's a dear little girl,

31

and she saved up so hard, and did so love the doll, and then the dog came and broke it. Now she's very, very unhappy. And dolls broken as much as that can't be mended. What am I to do to put it right? It really isn't fair, and I won't have it!'

Suddenly Mr Pink-Whistle knew what to do. He made himself appear suddenly, much to a small boy's surprise, and rushed into the toy-shop. He banged on the counter. The shop-woman appeared and looked surprised to see a fat little man wiping his green eyes with an enormous yellow handkerchief.

'Have you got another doll like the one the little girl bought just now?' he asked.

'Oh yes, of course,' said the shop-woman, and she lifted one out of the box. Mr Pink-Whistle snatched it up, slammed down the money, and tore out. The shop-woman really thought he was quite mad.

Jessie was walking home with her pram. She had put poor broken Rosemary Ann into it again, with her face towards the pillow, so that she couldn't see how broken she was.

Mr Pink-Whistle hurried up, and just as he got near, he dropped two or three pennies. They went rolling all over the place. 'Dear, dear!' said Mr Pink-Whistle, pretending to be vexed. 'Now where have they gone?'

'I'll get them for you,' said Jessie, just as he had known she would. She put her pram by the side of the pavement, and went to pick up the

pennies. As quick as lightning Mr Pink-
Whistle whipped the broken doll out of the
pram and put the new one in, face downwards.
He stuffed the broken one into one of his big
pockets, and covered up the other doll.

Soon Jessie came up to give him the pennies.
'What's the matter with your doll?' he asked.
'Why do you make her lie face downwards?'

'Because she's broken,' said Jessie, nearly
crying again.

'Now, how lucky that is!' said Mr Pink-
Whistle. 'I can mend broken dolls! Look! I just
tap her on the back of the head gently – like
this – and say "Hi-tiddle-hi-to, hi-tiddle-hi-to!"
And hey presto! – the doll will be all right
again!'

Jessie didn't believe him. She knew dolls weren't mended like that. But to please the funny little man she turned her doll over – and then she gave a scream.

'Rosemary Ann! You *are* all right! Your nose has come back! Your eyes are looking at me! You're quite, quite well! Oh, you darling! I'm so happy!' She snatched the doll out of the pram and hugged it as if she would squeeze it to bits. Mr Pink-Whistle felt all funny about the eyes again, and blew his nose loudly. This was fun! He'd put something right again! Good!

'Thank you ever so much,' said Jessie, her eyes shining with happiness. 'You must be magic!'

'I am, a bit,' said Mr Pink-Whistle, and his big ears waggled like a dog's and his green eyes gleamed. 'Well good-bye, little friend! Don't forget me, will you?'

'Oh, never!' said Jessie. 'I think you're really wonderful!'

So no wonder Mr Pink-Whistle skipped off as if he were treading on air. 'I've done it again! And I'll do it a third time before I'm much older! Yes, I certainly will!'

4

A marvellous afternoon

Jackie Brown was so excited that he could
hardly keep still. He kept hopping about, first
on one foot and then on another, till his mother
told him to go out into the garden and hop
there, on the smooth green grass.

'I shall be a grasshopper then!' said Jackie.
'Oh, Mother, I'm so excited! Tomorrow I'm
going to see the conjurer at the flower-show.
There's a great big tent there, and for sixpence
every one can go in and see the conjurer. I've
got sixpence and I'm going!'

'You've told me that about twenty times
already!' said his mother, laughing. 'Go along
out and play, and just think of something else
for a change!'

But Jackie couldn't think of anything else.
He had seen a conjurer once before, and the
magic things he did were so wonderful that the
little boy had never forgotten them. Fancy, he
even made a rabbit come out of an empty
glove! Jackie had known it was empty,
because it was his own glove that he had lent to
the conjurer!

'And tomorrow the conjurer will do lots
more magic!' said the little boy happily. 'Oh,
shan't I enjoy it!'

He saw Eileen and Dick next door, and he climbed over the wall to play with them. Dick had a new kite and he was trying to fly it. It was a lovely one.

The wind suddenly took it up very high, and Dick squealed with delight. 'Look at it!' he shouted. 'It's flying like a bird!'

But it didn't fly like a bird for long. The wind dropped and down came the kite — and it fell on top of the greenhouse! Dick tugged it. It was stuck tightly.

'Oh, bother!' he said. 'It's stuck! What shall I do?'

Jackie took the string and pulled gently. It was no use, the kite was held fast by something. 'Wait till the gardener comes, and he'll get a ladder and get it down for you,' he said.

'I did want to fly it this afternoon with Uncle Harry,' said Dick. 'He promised to take me to the hills.'

'Well, perhaps I can get it for you if the ladder isn't too heavy to carry,' said Jackie. He found the ladder, and the three children carried it carefully to the greenhouse. They set it up at the back, and Jackie went up the rungs.

He came to the kite. The string was wound round the spike at the top of the greenhouse. Jackie pulled hard, and then let go the top of the ladder to undo the string.

The ladder wobbled — the ladder fell! Crash! Jackie and the ladder reached the ground

together! Poor Jackie! He banged his head so hard on the ground that for a moment he couldn't get up. He felt queer. Then he sat up and held his head.

'You've cut your head on a stone,' said Eileen, frightened. 'It's bleeding. Come and show my mother, quickly.'

It was such a bad cut that Jackie had to have his head carefully bathed and bound up in a bandage. The little boy had had a bad shock, and his mother called in the doctor.

'The cut will soon heal,' said kind Doctor Henry. 'But he must be kept very quiet indeed for a day or two, Mrs Brown, to get over the shock. Put him to bed.'

'Oh, I can't go to bed – I can't, I can't!' wept poor Jackie. 'I want to see the conjurer tomorrow at the flower-show. Oh, please let me go!'

'I'm afraid you wouldn't enjoy yourself a bit, if you went all the way to the flower-show and back, with that dreadful aching head of yours,' said Doctor Henry. 'Be a good boy and lie quietly, and you'll soon be right. The conjurer will come again next year, I expect.'

'But next year is so far away!' wept Jackie, more disappointed than he had ever been in his life before. 'My head feels all right, really it does. Oh, I do want to go and see the conjurer! I'm so unhappy! All I did was to try and help Dick get his kite down – and now I've got a most unfair punishment, because I'm not to have my treat.'

'It's very bad luck, old man,' said the doctor. 'Very bad luck. But these things do sometimes happen, you know.'

'It shouldn't have happened when I was doing somebody a good turn,' wept Jackie.

'No, it shouldn't,' said the doctor. 'You

deserved a better reward than this!'

Poor Jackie! He was put to bed and there he had to stay. Dick and Eileen knew all about it next day, and they were very sad indeed. 'Just because he tried to get down my kite!' said Dick gloomily. 'It isn't fair.'

A small fat man, with queer big ears and bright green eyes like a cat's, was passing by when Dick said these words. He stopped at once.

'What isn't fair?' he asked.

Dick told him all about Jackie, and how he had hurt himself doing a kind deed, and now couldn't go to see the marvellous conjurer.

'He's very unhappy about it,' said Eileen. 'We've sent him some books to read, and I've lent him my best jig-saw puzzle – but I'm sure

he'll cry all the afternoon when the time comes for the flower-show.'

'Too bad, too bad!' said Mr Pink-Whistle – because, as you have guessed, he was the little fat man! 'I can't bear things like this, and I just won't have them. I shall put this right somehow!'

The two children stared in surprise at Mr Pink-Whistle. There was something very queer about him – and in a minute there was something even queerer still, because he just simply wasn't there! He had vanished before their very eyes!

'Where's he gone?' said Eileen in great surprise.

You would be surprised to know where he had gone! He had crept up to a rabbit-hole in the field nearby and had made a noise like a juicy carrot. Up came a tiny fat baby rabbit – and Mr Pink-Whistle caught it and put it into his pocket. Then he went back to Jackie's house. Nobody could see him, of course.

He climbed up a pipe and looked in at a window.

In the bedroom there was a small boy lying in bed with his head bandaged up, and tears rolling down his white cheeks. It was Jackie, feeling very unhappy because it was the afternoon of the flower-show and he couldn't go to see the conjurer.

Mr Pink-Whistle sighed. He hated to see anyone unhappy. He climbed quietly in at the

window and stood looking at Jackie.

'Hallo!' he said suddenly.

'Hallo!' said Jackie in surprise, looking all round to see where the voice came from. There wasn't anyone he could see at all.

'I'm a conjurer, come to do a few tricks for you,' said Mr Pink-Whistle.

'Good gracious!' said Jackie astonished. 'But where are you! I can't see you!'

'Well, you see, I'm so magic that I'm invisible at present,' said Mr Pink-Whistle. 'Now just tell me a few things you'd like to hop from the mantelpiece on to your bed, and they'll come!'

Jackie giggled. It was funny to think of things hopping from the mantelpiece to his bed. 'I'd like the clock to come,' he said. At once the clock seemed to jump from the mantelpiece and land on Jackie's bed! Of course, it was really Mr Pink-Whistle carrying it, but, as Jackie couldn't see him, it looked as if the clock came by itself!

Then a china pig flew through the air and back again. The coal-shuttle did a little jigging dance round the room, all by itself – though, of course, it was really Mr Pink-Whistle carrying it and jigging it about. But it did look so very funny!

Then Jackie's teddy-bear stood on the rail at the foot of his bed and danced a comical dance, sticking his legs out just as if he were doing steps! Jackie laughed till he cried. He couldn't see Mr Pink-Whistle's hands holding the bear. He thought the bear really was doing it!

'Now ask any of your toys to speak to you, and hear them talk!' cried Mr Pink-Whistle, thoroughly enjoying himself. It was so lovely to make somebody happy.

'Well – I'd like my old golliwog in that corner to say something to me,' said Jackie, sitting up in bed.

Mr Pink-Whistle, quite unseen, walked to where the golly was sitting. He made it wave its hand to Jackie, and then he talked for it, in a sort of woolly, golliwoggy voice.

'Hallo, Jackie! Get better soon!'

'Oh, Golly! I never knew you could talk before!' cried Jackie, very excited. 'Horsey, can you talk to me too?'

His old horse stood in the corner. Mr Pink-Whistle made it jiggle about, and then he spoke

for it. 'Nay-hay-hay-hay-ay! Nay-hay-hay-hay-ay! Hurry up and get better and ride on me, Jackie! Nay-hay-hay-hay-ay!'

Jackie was thrilled. 'You've got a lovely, neighing voice, Horsey!' he said. 'Oh, what fun this is! How magic you are, Mr Conjurer!'

'Pink-Whistle is my name,' said Mr Pink-Whistle politely. 'I'm glad you like the magic I do.'

'I only wish you could make a rabbit come out of somewhere, like the other conjurer did,' sighed Jackie. 'That was really most surprising magic.'

Mr Pink-Whistle felt the little baby rabbit in his pocket, and he was delighted that he had thought of bringing it.

'Where would you like the rabbit to come from?' he asked.

'Oh, out of my bed!' said Jackie. 'It would be lovely to have a rabbit in bed with me! And Mr Pink-Whistle, couldn't I see you please? You sound the kindest, nicest person I've ever heard.'

'Do I really?' said Mr Pink-Whistle, feeling very happy. 'I'm glad. Well – you *shall* see me, Jackie. Just look at the clock on the mantelpiece for one whole minute, and at the end of it, look at the foot of your bed. I'll be there!'

Now whilst Jackie was busily watching the clock, waiting till a minute had gone by, Mr Pink-Whistle carefully and quickly put the tiny rabbit into Jackie's bed, at the foot. Then he said the words that made him appear, and just as Jackie had counted the whole minute, there was Mr Pink-Whistle grinning away at him at the foot of the bed, his green eyes shining brightly.

'Oh! How nice and funny and jolly you are!' cried Jackie – and then he gave a squeal, because something was creeping up his bed. He put his hand down – and pulled out a baby rabbit!

'You're more magic than the other conjurer!' shouted Jackie. 'You really are! You're – you're . . . .'

And just then the door opened and Jackie's mother came in to see what the noise was. Mr

Pink-Whistle disappeared just in time.

'Look! Look! A conjurer has been here, and he made this rabbit come out of my bed!' squealed Jackie. 'Oh, I'm so happy! It's my very own rabbit for me!'

'But there's no conjurer here!' said Jackie's mother in astonishment, looking all round. And yet – the rabbit was certainly there. How very, very strange!

A little giggle came from the window, out of which Mr Pink-Whistle was quietly climbing. Down he went – and off into the world again to find something else to put right. Hurry, Mr Pink-Whistle!

5

The dog who lost his collars

Now once Mr Pink-Whistle had a rather queer adventure. It was with a little terrier dog.

The dog's name was Jinky, and it lived with its master and mistress in a nice little house in the town. Jinky was a friendly dog, and loved to welcome people, and he was always ready to put out his small red tongue to lick anyone.

But now, week after week, he was in disgrace. His mistress and master scolded him hard – and now he had been whipped. It was the first time, and he was very unhappy.

'You are a very bad little dog to keep losing your nice new collars!' his mistress said to him. 'You lost your first new red collar, and we bought you a green one with your name on it. You lost that the very next day! Then you had a fine brown one with bright studs all round it – and you came home without it the next week! And now you have lost the new blue one we gave you yesterday!'

'Woof!' said Jinky sadly.

'You are very naughty not to want to wear your collar,' said his master sternly. 'All dogs wear collars. So do their masters! You should be proud to be like your master! I can't

imagine how you get your collar off, you bad
dog – but just remember this, that you will be
whipped and locked up in your kennel every
time you do it!'

Jinky's master banged the kennel-gate and
left poor Jinky shut up inside. He was very sad.
He lay and whined pitifully. It wasn't fair! He
hadn't lost his collars! A horrid big boy had
taken them away from him each time! But he
couldn't tell his master that, because he could
only talk doggy language, and no two-legged
people understood it.

Just then somebody came by who *did*
understand whines and yelps and barks. It was
fat little Mr Pink-Whistle of course! He was
half a brownie, and his big pointed ears could
understand all that the birds and animals said,
just as the real brownies could.

So Mr Pink-Whistle could hear all that poor
Jinky was saying as he passed by the little
house. To you and to me it might have

sounded like 'Ooooo! Oooooo! Oooooo! Yelp, yelp, yelp! Oooooo! Oooooo!'

But to Mr Pink-Whistle it sounded like this:

'Oh, how sad I am! Oh, how unfair everything is! Oh, what a poor little dog I am, whipped for nothing! Oh, and how I love my master and mistress, and now I have made them very unhappy; but I couldn't help it, and they have made *me* unhappy too – but they *could* help it! Oh, tails and whiskers, I wish I wasn't a dog!'

Mr Pink-Whistle stopped and listened in astonishment. What could be the matter with the poor little dog? He made himself disappear and then he walked up the garden path and looked for the kennel. Inside was Jinky, his head on his paws, whining away to himself.

'What's the matter?' asked Mr Pink-Whistle in surprise. Jinky looked up. He couldn't see anyone, but he could smell somebody. How queer!

'It's all right,' said Mr Pink-Whistle, patting Jinky. 'I'm here, though you can't see me! Tell me, what's the matter?'

So Jinky told him his trouble. 'I'm being punished for something I didn't do,' he whined. 'But my master doesn't understand me when I try to tell him. A nasty, horrid boy keeps putting down lovely bones in the next street, and when I go to smell the bone, the boy pops out and catches me. Then he takes off my collar, and sends me home without it.'

'Well, what a wicked thing to do!' said Mr Pink-Whistle, very angry. 'And you've been whipped for that! Poor little dog, it's a shame! It's not fair! I must put it right.'

He undid the kennel-gate and Jinky slipped out of his kennel and out of the yard into the garden. 'Now you come along with me,' said Mr Pink-Whistle. 'We'll go and find this boy. Keep at my heels. You can smell them, even if you can't see them! We'll do to that boy a little of what he has done to you.'

Together they trotted down the street and round the corner. People meeting them only saw a small dog with a new collar round his neck – but Mr Pink-Whistle was there all right too! But he couldn't be seen.

'Look!' said the dog, stopping. 'There's a

lovely bone over there. I'm sure it's put there by that boy, so that I or any other dog shall go to it. Then he would catch us and steal our collars.'

'Well, you run up to it and smell it,' said Mr Pink-Whistle. 'Don't be afraid. I shall be near you.'

So Jinky ran up to the bone — and close beside him was Mr Pink-Whistle. As soon as Jinky reached the bone and sniffed at it, a big arm came over the fence and caught hold of the little dog. He was pulled right over the fence — and there behind the fence was a big boy with a horrid sly face.

'Another collar!' he grinned. But he didn't grin long! No — something most extraordinary happened!

Something took hold of him and wrenched at *his* collar! Something pulled at his tie. Something jerked at his coat — and before he could do anything to stop it, his collar, tie, and coat were taken right off him.

'Don't! What is it? Who is it? I can't see anyone!' cried the frightened boy. 'Go away! Go away!'

'I'm only doing to you what you've done to little dogs!' said a stern voice in his ear. 'Off with your shirt! Off with your boots! Off with your stockings!'

Off came everything except the boy's vest and trousers! Then a large fat hand spanked the boy well and set him howling loudly.

'Next time you think of stealing anything, just think of Mr Pink-Whistle!' hissed a voice in his ear. 'Yes – Mr Pink-Whistle! I'll come after you again and take your clothes away if you dare to steal another collar from a dog!'

'Mr P-p-p-p-pink-Whistle, please give me b-b-b-b-ack my clothes!' wept the boy. 'My mother will whip me if I go home without them.'

'Good!' said Mr Pink-Whistle. 'Very good. Go home and get whipped then!'

And the angry little man pushed the naughty boy so that he almost fell on to his nose. He ran off, howling and crying, wondering fearfully who Mr Pink-Whistle was. He couldn't see him – but he was there all right!

Mr Pink-Whistle went to the nearest dustbin

and stuffed the clothes in without being seen by anyone. Jinky licked his hand, after smelling about it for some time. The little dog thought Mr Pink-Whistle was wonderful.

'Now you go home, too,' said the fat little man, patting Jinky kindly. 'And don't be afraid of that boy any more. He's not likely to worry you or any other little dog again!'

Then off went Jinky very merrily, his tail in the air. Off went Mr Pink-Whistle too — and you may be sure that if he had had a tail it would have been straight up in the air as well, just like Jinky's!

6

A surprise for Dame Gentle

There was once an old woman called Dame Gentle, and she was just like her name. She was a dear old thing, and all the children loved her.

She was very poor, and sometimes, like Mother Hubbard, when she went to the cupboard – the cupboard was bare!

One day she had a bit of luck. Mrs Biddle wanted some scrubbing done, and she asked Dame Gentle if she thought she could do it.

'Of course!' said Dame Gentle. 'Haven't I rubbed and scrubbed all my life? A good bit of hard work never hurt anybody! I'll come along tomorrow and do whatever you want me to. Ah, I'm pleased about this, Mrs Biddle. I want a new blanket for my bed, and a new kettle for my stove. Maybe I'll be able to get them now!'

Well, she worked very hard indeed, and when the cleaning was done she had enough money to get what she wanted. She was very happy.

'Now for once in a way I'll give myself a real treat!' said old Dame Gentle. 'It's my birthday next week, and I'll make myself a cake, and get in a tin of cocoa to make some hot cocoa. I'll

boil the water in my new kettle, and I'll be warm at night under my new blanket. Ah, I'm in luck's way just now!'

She asked Mother Dilly to come and share the cake and the cocoa with her, for she was a generous old thing. When the day came, Dame Gentle ran out to ask one of her neighbours for a few flowers to put on her table.

And whilst she was gone, who should come to the open door but Mister Mean! He rapped. Nobody answered. He pushed open the door a bit wider and looked inside. Dame Gentle was not there!

Then Mister Mean saw the new cake on the table, the tin of cocoa, and the new blanket set out ready to show Mother Dilly when she came. His mean little eyes gleamed with delight. He tiptoed into the kitchen, put the cake and the cocoa into his pockets, and rolled

54

up the nice new blanket. He threw it over his
shoulder and ran out of the room and down
the path.

Just in time too – for Dame Gentle was
coming back with a few flowers for the table.
She trotted up the path to the front door, which
she had left open, and walked into her warm
kitchen.

'Mother Dilly will be here in a minute,' she
thought. 'I wonder if that kettle's boiling.'

And then she saw that her beautiful new
cake was gone! And the tin of cocoa! And the
lovely warm blanket!

Dame Gentle stared as if she couldn't
believe her eyes. *Where* had they gone to? She
looked all round. She looked in the cupboard –
but the cupboard was bare!

'Somebody's stolen them!' she said, and she

sank down into her chair. 'Oh, how mean! To steal from an old, old woman like me! My lovely cake – and my beautiful blanket – all gone! What a horrid thing to happen on my birthday!'

There was a knock at the door and Mother Dilly walked in. 'What's the matter?' she cried, when she saw how sad Dame Gentle looked.

'Somebody has stolen all my birthday things, that I worked so hard to get,' said Dame Gentle, wiping her eyes. 'It's upset me a bit.'

'What a shame!' said Mother Dilly, putting her arms round her friend. 'Oh, what a shame! Who stole them?'

'I don't know,' said Dame Gentle. 'I just ran out to get those flowers, and when I came back everything was gone – even the tin of cocoa!'

'Now don't you cry, dear,' said her friend. 'I'll just run home and get a bit of tea, and two pieces of shortbread that I've got left in my tin. And we'll eat those for your birthday.'

She left the old woman and hurried out into the street, really angry to think that someone should have treated old Dame Gentle so badly. She bumped into a fat little man with curious green eyes, as she ran out of the gate.

'Oh, I beg your pardon!' said Mother Dilly. 'I'm feeling rather hot and angry, and I didn't look where I was going.'

'Hot and angry!' said Mr Pink-Whistle in surprise, for of course it was the little secret

man who happened to be passing by. 'What's the matter?'

'Somebody has taken the cake, the cocoa, and the new blanket that my poor old friend, Dame Gentle, worked so hard to get,' said Mother Dilly fiercely. 'Isn't it a shame?'

'It certainly *is*!' said Mr Pink-Whistle, pricking up his ears at once. 'Is she a kind old soul?'

'The kindest in the world!' said Mother Dilly. 'She doesn't deserve such bad luck. I'm sure it's that horrid Mister Mean who has done this. He is such a sly creature, and not at all honest.'

'Really?' said Mr Pink-Whistle. 'Where does he live?'

'He lives at Cherry Cottage, round the corner,' said Mother Dilly. The little fat man raised his hat and ran off. Mother Dilly wondered who he was and what he was going to do.

Mr Pink-Whistle made himself disappear when he turned the corner. Then quite invisible, he looked for Cherry Cottage. Ah — there it was, at the end. He walked quietly up the path and looked in at the window.

Mister Mean was there, grinning away to himself. He had got the cake on the table, and had already eaten half of it. He had made himself a fine jug of hot cocoa from the cocoa powder in the tin, and he had draped the new blanket round himself to see how warm it was.

So of course Mr Pink-Whistle knew at once that Mister Mean was the thief. 'The mean, hateful creature!' he said to himself. 'Making an old woman unhappy, just when she had got a little treat ready. Ah, well, Mister Mean, you'll be sorry.'

Mr Pink-Whistle walked up to the door, gave it a loud crack with his fist and flung it open. He stamped in and made a sort of angry growling noise in his throat.

'Who's that?' cried Mister Mean in alarm, for he could see nobody, of course.

Mr Pink-Whistle said nothing. He just made the angry growling noise again. He went to the larder door and threw it open. It was full of goodies! There was a meat pie, a jam tart, a tin of biscuits, two kippers, a large tin of best tea, and some jars of potted meat. There was a big white loaf of bread in the bin and a pound of butter on a plate.

'Good!' Mr Pink-Whistle growled in his throat. 'Very good! I'll have those!'

He began to take them all off the shelves. Mister Mean, who was shivering in his shoes, jumped up at once. 'Stop thief!' he cried. 'Stop thief! Those are my belongings!'

Mr Pink-Whistle growled again. 'I'm only doing what you've just done this morning!' he said. 'Where did you get that cake from? Where did you get that blanket? You wicked fellow, to rob an old woman!'

Mister Mean was so terrified to hear a voice and not see anyone that he fell down on his knees and begged for mercy.

'Mercy!' shouted Mr Pink-Whistle, who was now beginning to enjoy himself. 'No! You shan't have any mercy. I might even eat you up!'

'Oh no, don't, don't! begged Mister Mean, who at once thought that Mr Pink-Whistle must be an invisible giant or something. He didn't know that he was a little man much smaller than he, Mister Mean, was! 'Take all you want – but leave my house and don't come back again. You frighten me! I can't see you! I'll never steal again, never, never, never!'

'Well, see you don't,' said Mr Pink-Whistle, 'or I shall certainly come back and gobble you up in one mouthful!'

Mr Pink-Whistle could hardly keep from giggling when he thought how difficult it would be for him to gobble up Mister Mean. He took the new blanket, and a new rug from the sofa, and set off to Dame Gentle's, carrying as well all the goodies he had found in the larder.

Mother Dilly hadn't yet come back. Dame Gentle had gone into the bedroom to wash her face. There was no one in the kitchen.

Mr Pink-Whistle draped the blanket over one chair and the rug over the other. He put the meat pie, the jam tart, the biscuits, kippers, tea, bread and potted meat on the table. Then, hearing footsteps, he slipped quietly to one side, and waited.

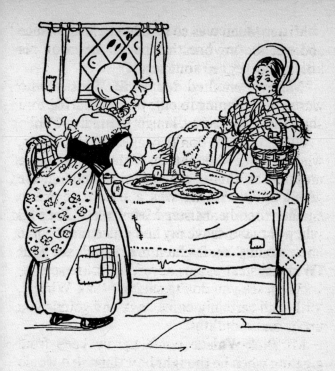

Dame Gentle came into the kitchen at the same time as Mother Dilly came back. They both saw all the new things at the same time. How they stared! They rubbed their eyes and stared again.

'Do you see what I see?' asked Dame Gentle at last. 'Goodies of all kinds! *And* my blanket and a new rug as well?'

'I see it all!' said Mother Dilly. 'It's very strange – but very pleasant. Let's sit down and eat!'

'Oh, I'm so happy again,' said Dame Gentle. 'Somebody was *very* unkind to me –

but now someone else has been even kinder! Blessings on him, whoever he may be! Blessings on his kind head!'

'Thank you,' whispered Mr Pink-Whistle, longing to show himself, but not daring to, in case he frightened the two old ladies. 'Thank you!'

'Funny!' said Dame Gentle, looking all round. 'I thought I heard something. IS ANYBODY HERE?'

But nobody answered. Mr Pink-Whistle had slipped out of the door, and was already on the way to his next adventure. Kind old Pink-Whistle!

7

The two ugly creatures

There was once a man that nobody loved. He lived alone in a cottage, and he was angry because he was blind.

He wore black glasses over his two blind eyes, and the children did not like these. So they were afraid of him, and the rudest of them called names after him, which was very unkind of them.

The man had always had weak eyes, but he had been so fond of reading that he had made them worse and worse. Now he couldn't see at all, and he was unhappy and angry. Angry because he knew that if only he had been wise, he would still have been able to see – and unhappy because he wanted to read, and couldn't, and because he had no friends.

People would have liked to be kind to him, but he wouldn't let them. He was bad-tempered, spiteful, and very, very lonely. His face grew uglier and uglier as he frowned more and more, and his black glasses seemed even blacker.

He used to go along the road of the town, tapping with his stick, and muttering to himself as he went, 'It isn't fair. I haven't anything at all! I've no friends. I've no books to read, no pictures to see. It isn't fair!'

And one day, of course, fat little Mr Pink-Whistle met him and heard him. What, something wasn't fair? Ah, Mr Pink-Whistle was all ears when he heard that, you may be sure.

'What isn't fair?' asked Mr Pink-Whistle, falling into step with the blind man.

'Go away,' said the blind man rudely. 'I never talk to anyone. Go away.'

'Then you must be very lonely,' said Mr Pink-Whistle in his gentlest voice.

'What's that to do with you?' said the blind man. 'I'm ugly, I know – even the children call out after me, the little wretches. And I'm bad-tempered. And I'm quite helpless, because I

can't see. I often fall off the kerb into the road –
but who cares? Nobody at all!'

'You are a very unhappy man,' said Mr
Pink-Whistle with a sigh. 'I wish I could find
you a friend. All you want is someone to love,
and someone who loves *you*.'

The blind man laughed loudly. 'Who would
ever love *me*?' he cried. 'If anyone sees me,
they run away. I know. I've heard them!'

'Let me help you across the road,' said Mr
Pink-Whistle, his heart very sad, for he could
not for the life of him think how he might put
things right for this poor man.

The blind man at first pushed away Mr
Pink-Whistle's hand – and then, because his
hand felt so friendly and so kind, he took it
after all, and allowed himself to be helped
across the road.

'Thanks for helping me,' he said. 'If I could
help you in return, maybe I would. But I can't
help anyone. I'm just no use at all.'

'You may be sure I'll ask you for help if you
can give it,' said Mr Pink-Whistle. 'Good-bye.
I'll come and see you again some time. You
live in that small house over there, don't you?'

'Yes,' said the blind man. 'Good-bye.' He
went off by himself, tapping with his stick.

Mr Pink-Whistle looked after him. 'It's not
fair,' he said. 'Some people have everything –
their eyes to see with, good health, friends, love
and happiness. And that poor man hasn't
anything at all, not even a friend. Yes – it's

mostly his own fault, and that only makes it worse!'

The little fat man looked quite sad for once. His eyes lost their twinkle and his mouth drooped. He stood thinking for a moment or two, and then he heard a yelping noise from round the corner. He ran to see what the matter was.

There was a pond round the corner. In it a wet dog struggled for his life. Mr Pink-Whistle waded in and got hold of him. The dog was tied to two big bricks.

'Good gracious!' said Mr Pink-Whistle, cutting the string that bound the dog to the bricks. 'Has someone been trying to drown you?'

'Woof!' said the dog, and as usual Mr Pink-Whistle understood all he said. 'Yes. The old

farmer who lives down the hill sent his man to drown me this morning.'

'How dreadful!' cried Mr Pink-Whistle, trying to dry the dog with his handkerchief. 'Why did he want to do that, little dog?'

'Well, you see,' said the dog sadly, 'I'm so ugly. Look at me and see. My head's too big. My tail is too long. My legs are too short. My ears droop down instead of up. And I'm such an ugly red colour. Everyone laughs at me when they see me, and really, I don't wonder. I saw myself once in a looking-glass outside a shop, and I laughed too.'

'It isn't fair,' said Mr Pink-Whistle, patting the dog. 'You've got a good heart, I am sure, and would be a splendid house-dog. That's all that really matters.'

'Oh, I would, I would!' barked the dog, and he licked Mr Pink-Whistle's hand with a long pink tongue. 'Couldn't you have me for your own? All the other puppies went to good homes, but nobody has ever wanted *me*.'

And then Mr Pink-Whistle had a wonderful idea. 'Listen!' he said. 'I know a poor, ugly, blind man, who is lonely and sad. He wants someone to love him and look after him — someone to sit with him in the evenings, and to guide him when he goes out for walks. He sometimes falls off the kerb, you know. Now do you think your heart is large enough to be this poor man's dog?'

'I would like it better than anything!' yelped

the dog. 'But won't he hate me, because I'm ugly?'

'He won't be able to see you,' said Mr Pink-Whistle. 'Come with me now, and we will see what happens.'

So the still-wet dog and the little fat man went to the cottage where the blind man lived. He was there, for he had just come in.

'Hallo!' said Mr Pink-Whistle, stepping into the parlour. 'I'm soon back again – and to ask your help too! I've got a poor little dog here, not much more than a puppy, that someone has tried to drown. Could I dry him by the fire, do you think?'

'I'll get a towel,' said the blind man, and he felt his way to a chest, pulled open a drawer and drew out a big brown towel. He went to the hearth-rug and knelt down. 'Where's the dog?' he said. 'I used to be fond of dogs, but now even they growl when they see me!'

The wet puppy put out his tongue and gently licked the blind man on the hand. He whined a little. The blind man began to dry him. 'You poor wet creature!' he said. 'So people are unkind to you too, are they? Well, there are two of us, then! Are you hungry? I've got some milk in the larder, and a bone too, I believe. Hey, you, there – would you get them?'

He was calling to Mr Pink-Whistle, but will you believe it, Mr Pink-Whistle didn't answer a word. No – he just stood by the door, smiling, and the blind man thought he had gone. Mr

Pink-Whistle wanted him to do as much as possible for the dog, for he knew that was the right way for them to make friends.

So the man fetched the milk and the bone. He found some biscuits too. He sat down by the fire and listened to the dog eating the food.

And then the puppy-dog jumped on to the man's knees, settled himself comfortably there, and licked the man's hands lovingly. Then he pushed his soft head against the man's face and licked his nose.

'Good dog, good fellow!' said the blind man, and he patted the dog. 'You don't mind how ugly and bad-tempered I am, do you? Well — I won't turn you out just yet. You can stay for a while.'

So the dog stayed. He shared the man's tea

with him. He found an old ball and rolled it over the floor. The man heard him playing and smiled for the first time for months. 'See you don't leave it for me to fall over,' he said. So the dog rolled it under the couch when he had finished.

'I don't think I can very well turn you out tonight,' said the blind man, when it was bedtime. 'I will keep you tonight, and when the man who brought you comes back, you shall go then.'

The dog went to sleep on the hearth-rug. But in the middle of the night he awoke and heard the blind man tossing and turning. He was always loneliest and unhappiest at night. The dog knew this at once, and he ran to the bed. He jumped up on to the eiderdown and snuggled down beside the man, his nose in the man's hand.

'Good fellow!' said the blind man, patting him. 'Good fellow!'

And do you know, when Mr Pink-Whistle came that way again, he saw the puppy-dog gambolling round happily, as fat as butter, and the blind man rolling a ball for him which the dog kept fetching and bringing back.

'Hallo!' said Mr Pink-Whistle.

'Hallo!' cried the blind man. 'You haven't come to fetch the dog have you? I couldn't do without him. You've no idea what a friend he is to me. He loves me and never leaves me for a minute. He guides me when I go out, and he

sleeps on my bed at night. He's the finest dog in the world!'

'And my master's the kindest, best man in the world!' yelped the dog. 'He belongs to me. I look after him and make him happy. He doesn't even know I'm ugly!'

'Good!' said Mr Pink-Whistle, looking at the happy face of the blind man, who was no longer ugly and bad-tempered. 'Very good! A little love and friendship go a very long way! Good-bye!'

8

The forgotten rabbits

In a nice big wooden hutch in a lovely garden lived two rabbits. Their names were Bubble and Squeak, and they were very pretty. Their ears were long and floppy, and their noses went up and down all day long.

They belonged to Winnie and Morris. At first the children had been most excited over their rabbits, and had brought them all kinds of delicious food every hour or two. Then they had grown used to them, and had cleaned their cage out and given them food once a day.

And now, lately, they had begun to forget all about them!

For two whole days the hutch had not been cleaned out! For two whole days the rabbits had had no fresh food.

Mother began to wonder if the rabbits were well looked after, and she went down to see. She was very angry when she found that their cage was so dirty and they had no food at all!

'I shall give the rabbits away,' she told Winnie and Morris. 'If you can't look after your own animals, you are not fit to have any.'

'Oh, don't do that,' said Winnie who really liked her rabbits, though she was lazy and couldn't be bothered to remember them. 'I'll clean out the hutch and feed them, really I will, Mummy.'

But she didn't. She remembered for three days, and then she forgot again. And this time

her Mummy was away and didn't see that the rabbits were forgotten! Auntie Jane was there to look after the children, and she quite thought that Winnie and Morris could be trusted to see to Bubble and Squeak.

The rabbits were hungry. They gnawed at their cage and tried to get out. They could see the green grass and they could see the cabbages in the kitchen-garden and the nice juicy lettuces. They felt as if they must get to them, somehow.

So they gnawed and they gnawed with their sharp teeth. And after three days, when they were so hungry that they could almost have eaten the wire netting, Bubble made a hole nearly big enough to squeeze through! But not *quite* big enough.

Poor Bubble! He tried to squash his soft body through the hole — and he stuck! He couldn't get forwards and he couldn't get backwards. It was really dreadful.

He began to squeal, and a rabbit squeal is a noise that makes everyone want to rush to its help. There was nobody in the house to hear, because the children and their aunt were out — but Mr Pink-Whistle heard.

He was walking at the end of the street, quite a long way away — but he heard the rabbit squealing, for he had ears that heard all cries of sadness and pain. He stopped and listened. He ran back down the road in a hurry, rushed into the front gate, round the house, and down the garden to where the rabbit-hutch was.

He soon saw what had happened to poor Bubble! He carefully cut the hole a little wider, took out the frightened rabbit, and placed it back in the hutch.

'Oh, thank you,' said Bubble, who knew at once that the little fat man was half a brownie.

Mr Pink-Whistle looked rather stern. 'You should not have tried to escape,' he said. 'That was a punishment to you, for trying to run away from a good hutch and kind owners.'

'Please, it isn't a good hutch, and Winnie and Morris are not kind,' said Bubble at once. 'Look — did you ever see such a dirty hutch and nasty hay? Can you see any food at all?'

Mr Pink-Whistle looked — and he frowned. 'No,' he said. 'There is no food at all — and the hutch is very dirty. Are Winnie and Morris unkind to you?'

'Oh yes,' said Squeak, her nose woffling hard, up and down, up and down. 'They often forget us. One day we shall die of hunger – and oh, it's dreadful to be hungry and yet see all that food out there, beyond our cage. That's why we tried to escape.'

'You poor, poor things!' said tender-hearted Mr Pink-Whistle. 'Children have no right to keep pets unless they look after them properly! This is a very wicked thing I hear!'

He opened the door of the cage wide. 'Come out, little rabbits,' he said. 'Go and eat all you want – and then run to the hills and live there in a burrow. I will not let these children keep you.'

The rabbits hopped out gladly. They rushed

to the lettuces, which grew in the children's own garden, and they ate the whole lot! They ate a row of new green pea-plants, and they nibbled the tops off the young turnips. Oh, they had a wonderful time! Then off they ran to the hills, and found a cosy burrow for the two of them.

Mr Pink-Whistle stared at the empty cage and his face was sad. 'What a lot of unfair things happen!' he said. 'Those were harmless, kindly little rabbits – and yet Winnie and Morris made them hungry, thin and miserable! Well, I've put things right for Bubble and Squeak – and now I must see to Winnie and Morris!'

He soon saw the children – bonny, fat and healthy, with rosy faces and shining eyes.

'People don't forget *your* meals!' he thought. 'You are chubby and fat. And *your* beds won't be dirty and smelly, unmade for days! No – they will be sweet and clean and fresh! My dear children, I have to teach you a lesson. You won't like it, but I cannot have you treating little creatures, smaller than yourselves, as unkindly as you have treated those two rabbits.'

Mr Pink-Whistle made himself disappear. He couldn't be seen at all. He went into the house and up the stairs, and soon found the children's rooms with their pretty white beds and blue eiderdowns.

Mr Pink-Whistle pulled all the bedclothes

off. He jumped on the white sheets with his dirty boots! What a mess he made of those two nice beds!

'Now the children will know what the rabbits felt like, having no nice clean cage to sleep in!' said Mr Pink-Whistle.

He went downstairs. Aunt Jane had placed two plates of delicious-smelling stew on the table for the children who had gone to wash their hands. Mr Pink-Whistle took the plates and emptied them out of the window! Then he put them back on the table.

What a to-do there was when Aunt Jane and the children came into the dining-room!

'How quickly you've eaten your dinner!' cried Aunt Jane.

'We haven't eaten *any* of it!' said Morris, staring in surprise at his empty plate, smeared with gravy.

'You must have,' said Aunt Jane. 'Your plates are empty. Don't tell naughty stories!'

'We're not!' said Winnie. 'Someone's eaten it instead of us. Can we have some more, Aunt Jane?'

'There isn't any,' said her aunt. 'You must have the pudding now. I simply can't understand it!'

Nor could the children. They were hungry and had so much wanted their stew. Aunt Jane went to get the pudding. It was a treacle pudding, and it sat upright on a big dish. Just as she set the dish on the table and turned round to get a spoon, Mr Pink-Whistle whipped the pudding off the dish and threw it out of the window!

Plonk! It landed on the grass and broke into bits. The children screamed in horror. 'Our pudding! It jumped off the dish!'

Aunt Jane hadn't seen what happened. She was very, very angry. 'You are being naughty children!' she cried. '*You* threw it out of the window – I know you did! It must have been you, for there's no one else here! Look at it there, smashed on the lawn! Go up to bed, both of you!'

Crying bitterly the two children went upstairs to bed – and then they saw their dirty, untidy beds, with the clothes on the floor. They

called their aunt, and she looked at the mess in dismay.

'We didn't do it, really we didn't,' sobbed Winnie. 'Please believe us, Aunt Jane.'

Aunt Jane didn't know what to think. She made the beds, and told the children to get undressed. Winnie went to a drawer of her chest as soon as her aunt had gone. 'I've got some biscuits and chocolate here, Morris,' she said. 'Let's have them. I'm so hungry!'

But as soon as she opened her drawer, Mr Pink-Whistle's invisible hand went in, and he took out the packet of biscuits and the bar of chocolate. He threw them out of the window.

The children screamed with rage and fright. Whatever could be happening! Then Mr Pink-Whistle pulled their beds to pieces again and jumped on the sheets!

'Who is it? Who is it? It's someone we can't see!' wept Winnie.

'Yes,' said Mr Pink-Whistle. 'But now you *shall* see me!' He muttered some very magic words – and hey presto! there he was, standing in front of the children, a little fat man with pointed brownie ears and large green eyes.

'Good morning!' he said. 'I'm sorry to behave like this – but for the sake of Bubble and Squeak I have to put things right. You forgot to clean their bed – so I've made your beds dirty and untidy to show you how horrid it is. You forgot to give them food and they went hungry. So I've taken away your food to show you what it's like to be really hungry. What do you think about it?'

'I'm ashamed,' said Winnie, and she hung her head.

'I'm sorry about it,' said Morris, and he went red. 'I'll go straight down to the hutch now and give the rabbits a good feed.'

Off went the children – and found the hutch empty. How they cried!

'It's a hard lesson,' said Mr Pink-Whistle, feeling sad. 'But learn it, my dears, and you'll be happier in the future – and so will your pets. Good-bye!'

He disappeared. Where had he gone? The children couldn't imagine!

9

Jimmy's day in the country

It was going to be a very exciting day for fifty of the town children. They were all to go for a day in the country. How lovely!

At ten o'clock a big red bus stood waiting at the corner of the road, and the fifty children climbed in with two grown-ups to look after them. Off they went, singing and laughing.

Each child had his lunch with him and his tea, in school-bags. Jimmy had egg sandwiches, two slices of cake, and an apple for his lunch; and jam sandwiches, two buns, and a piece of chocolate for his tea. He thought it was lovely.

'Now, listen,' said Miss White, one of the grown-ups, when at last the bus arrived at a farm in the country. 'You may all wander off as you please, and see all the animals on the farm – but be sure not to go out of reach of the bell, because the bus will take us back at five o'clock, and you must all be here then. I shall ring the bell at half-past four to warn you.'

The children ran off, talking happily. Some went to see the pretty new calves. Some ran to see the ducks and the hens. Others begged for a ride on the old brown horse, and Jimmy waited

for his turn too. He had been in the country
before and he loved it.

Very soon he felt hungry, and he found a
sunny place beneath a hedge and sat down to
eat his lunch. Oooh! How good the egg
sandwiches were! The cake was delicious, and
the apple was as sweet as sugar.

'I musn't eat my tea as well now, though I'd
very much like to!' said Jimmy, looking at his
jam sandwiches. 'No – I'll leave them till four
o'clock.'

He packed up his bag again, put it over his
shoulder, and went off across the fields to see if
he could find some flowers to take home to his
mother.

He knew his way about very well, for he had
been down to the farm before. He jumped over

a little stream, crossed two fields, and went into a wood. Big pink flowers were growing there, and Jimmy began to make a bunch of them. He went right through the wood, and came out at the other side. There was a field that used to have goats in.

'I wonder if the goats have any babies,' thought Jimmy to himself. 'I love little kid-goats!'

He went to see – and there, under the hedge, he saw a small girl, with tears rolling down her cheeks. She belonged to Jimmy's party, and he looked at her in surprise.

'Whatever's the matter?' he asked.

'It's those horrid goats,' sobbed the small girl, whose name was Margery. 'I came here, and lay down in the sunshine, and somehow I

fell asleep. And two big goats came whilst I was asleep and ate all my lunch – yes, and my tea too. And they even ate my bag as well! This is all that's left of it – look!'

She showed him the strap. Jimmy was sorry for her. 'It must be dreadful to have your lunch and your tea both eaten by goats,' he thought.

'Have you eaten your lunch?' asked Margery, looking at his bag hungrily. 'I suppose you couldn't share it with me?'

'I've eaten it,' said Jimmy. And then, because he was a kind boy, he said, 'But you can have my tea if you like! My mother will give me some more when I get home!'

'Oh, thank you!' said Margery – and she ate up every scrap of Jimmy's nice tea – chocolate and all!

'Now I'll take you where there are wild strawberries,' she said. 'I found them last year in the wood.'

But although they hunted for ages and ages they couldn't find any at all. 'It's time for the bell soon, I should think,' said Jimmy. 'Don't let's go too far.'

When the bell rang at half-past four, Jimmy was dreadfully hungry – but his tea was inside Margery! So he couldn't have any! 'Come along,' he said. 'We must go back. The bus will be there.'

So back they went – but Margery was tired and couldn't hurry. And then she fell down and hurt her knee so badly that she howled and howled! Jimmy bathed her knee in some water and tied it up with his handkerchief. Then he tried to hurry Margery along, but she could only limp very slowly, for her knee hurt her.

'We shall miss the bus!' cried Jimmy in despair. 'Do hurry!'

Margery cried. She fell over again. Jimmy knelt down and made her get on his back. 'I'll give you a piggy-back,' he said. 'Maybe we'll be quicker then.'

But Margery was heavy and he couldn't carry her for long. 'Let's sit down here and wait for the bus to go by,' said Margery at last. 'We can stop it then.'

So they sat down – but, alas, for them! the bus went another way, and they saw it turning a corner far down the hill, full of children going home!

'Oh, it's too bad!' cried Jimmy, almost in tears. 'I've helped you all I could, Margery, and given you my tea and carried you – and now we've missed the bus and my mother will be worried.'

'Look – here's someone coming,' said Margery. They looked down the lane, and saw a fat little man. It was Mr Pink-Whistle, of course, and he was going home for a little holiday. He had been away from his cottage and his cat, Sooty, for quite a long while.

He saw the children and stopped. 'What's the matter?' he asked.

Margery told him all their story. 'It's too bad for poor Jimmy,' she said. 'He did help me such a lot, and he was so kind – and now I've made him miss the bus and we haven't any money and we've got to walk home, and my knee hurts, and . . . .'

'Good gracious me!' said Mr Pink-Whistle. 'How very lucky that I happened to walk down this way. I'll soon put things right! That's what I'm made for, I think – to put things right. But you wouldn't believe what a lot of things go wrong! I'm always hard at work, every single day.'

'I like you,' said Margery, and she put her small hand into Mr Pink-Whistle's rather large one. 'You look a bit like a brownie in my picture-book at home. But how can you put things right for us? There isn't another bus home.'

'Oh yes, there is,' said Mr Pink-Whistle. 'It's not the usual bus, you know – it's one that nobody sees but the little folk of the woods! But if you'd really like to see it, just put on these glasses, will you? They will help you.'

He handed the two surprised children a pair of glasses each. They set them on their noses and looked through them.

My goodness! What a marvellous surprise! They could see small brownies peeping at them from the hedge. They could see tiny folk of all sorts running here and there, no bigger than flowers. And they could see a queer little cottage standing not far off, which they were quite certain hadn't been there before!

'It *was* there before,' said Mr Pink-Whistle, 'but you hadn't got those magic glasses on, so you just didn't see it! A friend of mine lives there. Let's see if she will give us tea.'

They went up to the little green door. Rat-tat! The door opened and a small woman stood there, with big pointed ears just like Mr Pink-Whistle's. Her eyes were green too, like his. She beamed all over her face and cried, 'Mr Pink-Whistle! What a lovely surprise! You're just in time for tea. Do come in!'

So they all went in, and Mr Pink-Whistle told his friend, Dame Little, all about Jimmy and Margery. They sat down to tea – and, my goodness, what a tea it was! There were wild strawberries and cream. There were little biscuits shaped like flowers. There were cakes shaped like animals, and they were full of cream. The funny part about them was that when you pressed them, each cake squeaked! But Jimmy didn't squeeze too hard, because it

shot the cream out! What a tea it was!

'The bus will be by soon,' said Dame Little. So they shook hands with her, and she took them to her gate. Down the lane came the bus – but what a bus! It was shaped like a Noah's ark on wheels, and you had to climb up a ladder and get in at the lid, which the conductor held open!

Inside there were rows of seats, and on them sat rabbits, moles, a hedgehog, brownies, and many other passengers. They looked rather surprised to see the children, but made room for them most politely. The strange bus started off and the conductor shut the lid.

'This is a most surprising adventure,' said Jimmy. 'I can't believe it's true.'

'Well, you don't need to believe it,' said Mr

Pink-Whistle, laughing. 'Think it's a dream, if you like – it will be just as exciting, either way!'

The bus stopped at the end of the children's street, and they got out, yawning. 'Thank you very much, Mr Pink-Whistle,' began Jimmy, But Mr Pink-Whistle was gone – and so was the bus.

'*Was* it a dream, do you think?' said Margery to Jimmy. 'I wish I knew!'

'Well, all I can say is that I'm jolly glad I helped you, Margery,' said Jimmy. 'I'd never have had this lovely adventure if I hadn't!'

10
The mean little boy

There was once a mean little boy called Wilfrid. He took other children's toys away and wouldn't give them back. He pinched the little girls when no grown-up was about. He hit the little boys, and sometimes threw their caps right up into the trees so that they couldn't get them.

Wilfrid was big and rather strong for his age, and it wasn't much good trying to stop him. All that the other children could do was to run away when they saw him.

But one day little Janet didn't run away quickly enough. She was playing with her tricycle in the street and Wilfrid saw her. He loved riding on tricycles because he hadn't got one himself – so up he ran and caught hold of the handle.

'Get off, Janet. I want a ride,' said Wilfrid.

'No,' said Janet. 'You are much bigger than I am, and my mother says I musnt't let bigger children ride my little tricycle in case they break it.'

'Well, I'm jolly well going to ride it!' said Wilfrid. He dragged Janet off her tricycle and she fell on the ground. Wilfrid was always so rough. Then he got on the little tricycle himself and rode off quickly down the street, ringing the bell loudly.

My word, how quickly he went! You should have seen him. All the other children skipped out of the way, and even the grown-ups did, too. Ting-a-ling-a-ling! went the bell – ting-a-ling-a-ling!

Wilfrid came to where the street began to go down a little hill. On he went, just as fast – and then he came to a roadway. He tried to stop, but he couldn't. Over the kerb he went, crash! The tricycle fell over, and Wilfrid fell too.

He didn't hurt himself – but the tricycle was quite broken! The handle was off, the bell was spoilt and wouldn't ring, and one of the pedals was broken!

A little fat man with pointed ears and green eyes saw the accident. It was Mr Pink-Whistle of course, trotting along as usual to see what bad things in the world he could put right.

He hurried up to the boy who had fallen, meaning to pick him up and comfort him, but before he could get there a little girl ran up and began to scold him, crying bitterly all the time.

'You horrid boy, Wilfrid! Now you've broken my tricycle and I did love it so much. My mother will be very angry with me because you rode it. I shan't be able to get it mended, and it will have to be put away in the shed and never ridden any more!'

And Janet cried bucketfuls of tears all down herself till her dress was quite damp. The other children came running up to see what had happened. They glared at Wilfrid, who made a face and slapped Janet because she cried so loudly.

'It's a silly tricycle anyway!' said Wilfrid. 'Stupid baby one. Good gracious, I might have broken my leg, falling over like that!'

He stalked off, whistling, leaving the others to pick up the tricycle and to comfort poor Janet.

'Horrid boy!' said Tom. 'Don't cry, Janet.'

'Yes, but it isn't fair!' wept Janet. 'It's *my* tricycle, and he took it away from me – and now it's broken and my mother will be so cross.'

Mr Pink-Whistle was sorry for the little girl. He walked up to the children and patted Janet's golden head.

'Now, now, don't cry any more,' he said. 'Maybe *I* can mend your tricycle. Tell me some more about the boy who broke it.'

Well, you should have heard the things that came pouring out about Wilfrid, the mean boy! Mr Pink-Whistle didn't care whether it was telling tales or not – he just *had* to know about him. And soon he knew so much that a big frown came above his green eyes and he pursed up his pink mouth.

'Hmmmm,' said Mr Pink-Whistle, deep down in his throat. 'I must see into this. That boy wants punishing. But first we will mend your tricycle, little girl.'

Well, Mr Pink-Whistle took the broken tricycle along to a bicycle shop, and soon it

was as good as new. The handle was put on
again very firmly. A new bell was bought and
fixed on. It was much better than the other one.
The pedal was nicely mended – and then Janet
got on her tricycle and rode off in delight.

'Oh, thank you!' she cried. 'But I do hope I
don't meet Wilfrid! He will want to ride my
tricycle again and break it!'

'I'll look after Wilfrid!' said Mr Pink-
Whistle. And then, in his very sudden and
extraordinary way, he disappeared! One
minute he was there – and the next he wasn't.
But really and truly he *was* there – but quite

invisible, because, as you know, he was half magic.

He had seen Wilfrid coming along again — and Mr Pink-Whistle meant to watch that small boy and see all the things he did! Yes — Wilfrid wasn't going to have a very good time now.

Wilfrid strolled along, hands in pockets, making faces at children he met. When he met Kenneth, who was eating a rosy apple, Wilfrid stopped.

'Give me that apple!' he said.

'No!' said Kenneth, putting the apple behind his back. Wilfrid snatched at it — and it rolled into the mud so that nobody could eat it at all!

Kenneth yelled. Wilfrid grinned. Mr Pink-Whistle frowned. The little fat man bought another apple at the fruit-shop and slipped it into Kenneth's pocket without being seen. He would find it there when he got home — what a lovely surprise!

Then Mr Pink-Whistle suddenly became visible again, and walked into a shop. He bought several rather large sheets of white paper, some pins, and some black chalk. He stood by a wall and quickly wrote something in big letters on a sheet of paper.

Then he disappeared suddenly — but a very strange thing happened. On Wilfrid's back a large sheet of white paper suddenly appeared, and was gently pinned there so that Wilfrid didn't know. On the paper was written a single

sentence in big black letters: 'I KNOCKED
KENNETH'S APPLE INTO THE MUD!'

Well, Wilfrid went along the street humming
gaily, not knowing that anything was on his
back at all. But very soon all the children knew
it. First one saw it, then another — and soon a
big crowd was following Wilfrid, giggling hard.

Wilfrid heard them and turned round.

'What's the joke?' he asked.

'*You're* the joke!' said Harry.

'You stop giggling and tell me *how* I'm the
joke!' said Wilfrid fiercely.

'Who knocked Kenneth's apple into the
mud?' called Jenny

'How do you know I did?' cried Wilfrid. 'I
suppose that baby Kenneth has been telling
tales. Wait till I see him again!'

'No he hasn't told us — you told us yourself,
giggled Doris.

'I didn't,' said Wilfrid.

'Look on your back!' shouted Lennie.

Wilfrid screwed his head and looked over his shoulder. He caught sight of something white on his back. He dragged at his coat and pulled off the paper. He read it and went red with rage.

'Who dared to pin this on my back!' he shouted. 'I'll shake him till his teeth rattle!'

Everyone shook their heads. No – they hadn't pinned the paper on Wilfrid's back, though they would have liked to, if they had dared.

Wilfrid threw the paper on to the ground and stamped on it. 'If anyone does that to me again, they'll be sorry for themselves!' he said fiercely. 'So just look out!'

But the one who had done it didn't care a rap for Wilfrid's threat. No – old Pink-Whistle grinned to himself and trotted quietly along after Wilfrid, waiting to see what mean thing the boy would do next.

And then out would come another sheet of paper, of course – and Wilfrid would have to wear another notice on his back.

11

Wilfrid has a good many shocks

Mr Pink-Whistle followed Wilfrid home, and
then he sat on the wall outside, still invisible, to
wait for him to come out. Inside the house he
could hear Wilfrid being very rude to his
mother.

'Wilfrid, I want you to run down and get me
some potatoes,' said his mother.

'I don't want to. I'm tired,' said the selfish
boy.

'Now you do as you're told, Wilfrid,' said
his mother. 'Hurry up.'

'Shan't!' said Wilfrid. 'I'm tired, I tell you.'

Mr Pink-Whistle listened, quite horrified. To
think that any boy could talk to his mother like
that! It was simply dreadful. Wilfrid went on
being rude – and then, when his mother had
gone to the back door to speak to the baker,
Wilfrid slipped out of the front door. *He* wasn't
going to go and fetch potatoes, not he!

Mr Pink-Whistle had been busy writing
something on a sheet of white paper with his
black chalk. He waited till Wilfrid passed him,
and then the little fat man neatly pinned the
paper on to Wilfrid's back. He did it with such
a magic touch that the boy didn't feel anything

at all. Off went Wilfrid down the street, whistling – and on his back the sheet of paper said: 'I HAVE BEEN VERY RUDE TO MY MOTHER!'

Well, it wasn't long before all the passers-by saw the paper and began to laugh at it. 'Fancy!' they said to one another, 'he has been rude to his mother! Well, he certainly looks a most unpleasant boy, it's true – but fancy being rude to his *mother*!'

The other children soon saw the notice and gathered round, giggling. Wilfrid glared at them. Whatever was all the giggling about?

'You've been rude to your mother!' shouted Kenneth.

'Bad boy! You've been rude to your mother!' yelled all the children.

Wilfrid stopped in surprise. Now how in the world did the others know that? He hadn't told anyone – and his mother certainly hadn't, for she would be too much ashamed of her son to say such a thing.

'How do you know?' he demanded angrily.

'You've got it on your back,' shouted the children in glee.

Wilfrid tore the paper off his back and looked at it. How he scowled when he saw what was printed there! But how could it have got on his back? And who could have written that sentence?

He tore the paper into little pieces and stuffed them into a litter bin. Then he stamped

I HAVE BEEN VERY RUDE TO MY MOTHER

off angrily. Just wait till he caught anyone pinning paper on his back again! He kept turning round quickly to make sure that no one was creeping behind him.

Soon he met Alison, and she had a bag of sweets. 'Give me one!' said Wilfrid.

'No,' said Alison bravely. Wilfrid gave her such a pinch that she squealed loudly and ran away, hugging her bag of sweets and crying.

Well, you can guess that it wasn't more than half a minute before Mr Pink-Whistle had pinned another sheet of paper on Wilfrid's back! This time it said, in bold black letters: 'I HAVE PINCHED ALISON AND MADE HER CRY.'

Everyone who saw it looked surprised – and then grinned. 'What a nasty little boy that must be!' they thought. They wondered if he knew that he had the paper on his back. He didn't know at first – but as soon as he met some other children, he knew at once!

For they danced around him, shouting, 'You pinched Alison! You horrid boy! You pinched Alison and made her cry!'

'How do you know?' shouted Wilfrid. 'Did she tell tales of me?'

'No – you're telling tales about yourself!' yelled back the children, keeping a good distance away from the angry little boy. He at once felt round at his back and tore off the paper. When he read what was written he was rather frightened. He felt quite certain that no one had been near enough to him to pin on that paper – he had been keeping a good watch. Then how did it get on his back?

Wilfrid thought he would go home. He didn't like these queer happenings at all. It wasn't a bit funny suddenly to have horrid things pinned on his back for people to laugh at. He ran home quickly.

His mother was out in the garden. Wilfrid thought that no one else was in the house, so he crept to the jam cupboard, and looked for a pot of strawberry jam. He didn't know that Mr Pink-Whistle was just behind him, quite invisible! The naughty boy ran off with the jam and sat down under a bush in the front garden to enjoy it.

Mr Pink-Whistle busily wrote on another sheet of paper, then sat down beside Wilfrid,

and pinned it gently on his back. The boy couldn't see Mr Pink-Whistle, of course, and he was so busy with the jam that he didn't even hear the very slight rustle of the paper.

He finished the jam and went indoors, and as soon as he turned round his mother saw what was pinned on his back: 'I HAVE STOLEN A POT OF STRAWBERRY JAM.'

'Oh, *have* you!' said Wilfrid's mother, and she went to her jam cupboard to look. Sure enough a pot was gone.

'Wilfrid! You bad boy! You've taken my jam!' she cried. 'Go straight upstairs to bed and stay there for the rest of the day! Go quickly before I smack you!'

Wilfrid rushed upstairs, for his mother was really very angry indeed. He took his coat off to undress – and saw the notice that said so plainly, 'I HAVE STOLEN A POT OF STRAWBERRY JAM.'

Wilfrid stared at it, frightened. Who had seen him take the jam? Who had pinned that notice on him? It was magic. It couldn't be anything else. Wilfrid began to cry.

'Oh, it's all very well to cry,' said the voice of Mr Pink-Whistle in the bedroom. 'You cry just because you are frightened – not because you are sorry. You are a very horrid, rude and mean little boy.'

'Oh, who's speaking to me?' asked Wilfrid, staring all round the room and seeing nobody.

'I'm so frightened. Please, please, don't pin any
more notices on me. I can't bear it.'

'I shall go on pinning notices on you just as
long as you do things that deserve it,' said Mr
Pink-Whistle. 'I say again — you are a very
horrid, rude and mean little boy.'

There was a silence. Mr Pink-Whistle had
gone. Wilfrid slowly got undressed and
climbed into bed. He lay there with nothing to
do, thinking very hard.

Yes — the strange voice was right. He was a
horrid boy. He had spoilt Kenneth's apple —
broken Janet's tricycle — been rude to his
mother — stolen her pot of jam — pinched
Alison — good gracious, what a long list of
horridness!

107

'If only I could put things right!' thought Wilfrid uncomfortably. 'It's so easy to do something wrong — and so difficult to put it right afterwards.'

His mother came into the room, very angry. Wilfrid called to her, 'Mother! I'm sorry I was rude today — and please forgive me for taking the jam. I never will again. Can I take some money out of my money-box and buy another pot for you?'

'Well — that would be very nice of you and would put everything right again, Wilfrid,' said his mother, surprised and pleased. 'You can get up and go and buy it now, before you change your mind.'

'I shan't change my mind,' said Wilfrid, and he hurriedly dressed again. He had been saving

up to buy a big bow and some arrows — but never mind! He tipped all the money out of his box. There were seven shillings, a sixpence, and many pennies. He put it all into his pocket.

He rushed out. He went to the grocer's and bought a large pot of best strawberry jam. He went to the greengrocer's and bought two apples for Kenneth. He went to the toy-shop and bought a doll for Alison, and a tricycle basket for Janet. All his money was spent!

The other children were most astonished when they saw Wilfrid coming along looking ashamed and shy! He was always so bold and rude!

'Kenneth — here's something for you,' said Wilfrid, and he pushed the apples into the boy's hands. 'Alison — I didn't mean to hurt

you and make you cry. Here's a doll to make up for it. And, Janet – here's a new basket to put on the front of your tricycle. I'm sorry I broke it.'

'Oh, Wilfrid!' cried all three children in the greatest delight. 'How nice of you! Thank you very much.'

Wilfrid went red and ran home with the jam. He gave it to his mother and she kissed him.

'There's nobody can be nicer than you when you really try!' she said.

'Really, Mother?' said Wilfrid, feeling very happy all of a sudden. 'Oh, Mother – I don't know how those horrid notices came on my back, but I do hope there won't be any more, now I've tried to put things right!'

Well – there was one more! Mr Pink-Whistle had watched Wilfrid trying to put

110

things right, and he was pleased. He followed the boy about for a few more days and saw that he really was trying to be better. So he put one more notice on Wilfrid's back – and then went off to another town to see if he could find something else to put right.

What was on that last paper? Something that Wilfrid didn't mind at all! It said: 'I REALLY HAVE BEEN DOING MY BEST!'

And all the children clapped their hands and cried, 'Yes, Wilfrid – you have!'

2. Mr Pink-Whistle Interferes

A Beaver Book
Published by Arrow Books Limited
62–65 Chandos Place, London WC2N 4NW
A division of Century Hutchinson Limited
London Melbourne Sydney Auckland
Johannesburg and agencies throughout
the world

First published in 1950
Revised edition published in 1970 by
Dean and Son Limited
Beaver edition 1981
Reprinted 1984, 1987 and 1988
© Copyright Enid Blyton 1950
© Copyright Darrell Waters Limited 1970

Enid Blyton is the Registered Trade Mark
of Darrell Waters Limited

Set in Times
Printed and bound in Great Britain by
Cox & Wyman Ltd, Reading

ISBN 0 09 954200 5

Contents

1

Mr Pink-Whistle interferes

I hope you remember dear old Pink-Whistle, the little man who is half a brownie, and has pointed ears? He can make himself invisible if he wants to, and he goes about the world trying to put wrong things right.

One day Mr Pink-Whistle walked into the village of Little-Trees. There was a market there, and he wanted to buy some fish for Sooty, his cat. In the middle of the market were three stalls, and one man and his wife ran all of them.

One was for groceries, one was for fruit and vegetables, and the third one was for fish. Mr Pink-Whistle looked at the man who was serving at the fish-stall, and he didn't much like what he saw.

'What a nasty-looking fellow!' thought Pink-Whistle. 'What a toothy smile – and what horrid little eyes, set so close together that they're almost touching! And his wife isn't much better.'

He didn't think he wanted to go and buy anything from the fish-stall, but it seemed to be the only one there. So he went up to buy.

'Who's the man who runs these stalls?' he asked an old dame next to him.

'It's Tom Twisty and his wife,' said the old woman. 'Like name, like nature, I say! We never seem to get our proper weight of goods, or the right amount. But everyone's afraid of Tom Twisty. He owns half the houses in our village, and once he turned one of us out because we dared to complain about his goods.'

Mr Pink-Whistle watched Tom Twisty carefully. He was counting out some oranges for a little girl. 'Let me see, you want twenty. Hold out your basket. That's right. Now – one, two, three – oh, that nearly rolled out, didn't it? Five, six, seven – wait a bit, that's a bad one – oh, no, it isn't – nine, ten, eleven, twelve – how's your mother today, dear? Better, I hope. Fifteen sixteen, seventeen – will there be enough room in the basket? Ah, yes – nineteen, twenty!'

Well, I don't know if you have managed to see how Tom Twisty cheated the little girl out of five oranges, but he certainly did. If you read his little speech again, you will soon find out! She paid him for twenty oranges and went off with only fifteen in her basket!

Mr Pink-Whistle was smart, and he saw at once that Tom Twisty had cheated the little girl. He stood still and watched, getting very angry indeed.

He saw Tom Twisty weigh out two pounds of flour, but Mr Pink-Whistle was quite sure there were *not* two pounds there. He saw him empty eight pounds of potatoes into somebody's basket – but quite a pound of dirt

8

went in with them too, and was paid for as potatoes. Dear, dear, dear — what a rogue Twisty was, to be sure!

Mr Pink-Whistle went up for his fish. He asked for two pounds, and Tom Twisty's wife served him. She was not all smiles like her husband — she was a sulky-looking woman. She slapped the fish down in her scales, and although Mr Pink-Whistle was sure that it did not weigh two pounds, down tipped the fish to one side, balancing the pound weights the other side.

'Is that really *two* pounds?' said Pink-Whistle. The woman glared at him.

'How dare you say I'm cheating you!' she cried in a shrill voice.

'I'm not saying that you are,' said Pink-Whistle, in a mild sort of voice. 'I just asked

9

you if that was really *two* pounds? I want to
know.'

Mrs Twisty picked up the fish and threw it
straight at Mr Pink-Whistle. It knocked his hat
off. He picked up the fish, wrapped it in a bit of
paper, paid for it, raised his hat, and went off
without a word. Mrs Twisty stared after him.

'I'll get the policeman here next time you
come!' she yelled after him. 'That I will.
Accusing honest people of cheating! Ho, you
wait till next time!'

Mr Pink-Whistle slipped into a shop. The
shopman was a friend of his and nodded to
him. 'May I use your scales for a moment?'
asked Pink-Whistle politely, and popped his
packet of fish on the scales there. He put a two-
pound weight on the other side. Down it went,
and Mr Pink-Whistle stared solemnly.

'That fish can only weigh about a pound and
a half,' he said. 'Yet I saw that it went down on
the scales with a bump when it was weighed
before – and I paid for two pounds.'

'You've been to old Twisty's stalls!' said his
friend. 'He's a bad lot, and so is his wife.
Cheating all the time. But he's rich and
powerful and people are afraid to complain.
They say he is friendly with the policeman too
– pays him to keep away from the market
when he's there with his stalls.'

'Hum!' said Mr Pink-Whistle. 'Well, well!
What a shame to cheat all the little girls and
old women and busy housewives. I've a good
mind to put this right.'

'Don't you meddle with Twisty,' said his

10

friend. 'He'll get the better of you. He's as sharp as a bagful of monkeys.'

'Well, maybe I'm as sharp as *two* bags full,' said Pink-Whistle, with one of his big grins. 'Thank you for the use of your scales, friend. Good-bye.'

Now Mr Pink-Whistle was quite determined to look very closely at the scales and the weights on Tom Twisty's stall, so he went back in the dinner-hour and waited for Twisty and his wife to leave for a meal.

But they didn't. They sat and ate their dinner close by their stalls. Still, that didn't worry Pink-Whistle much. He decided to make himself invisible and do a little examining of the scales without being seen.

In a trice the little man had disappeared. He was quite invisible! He walked over to the three stalls and began to examine a pair of scales. He tipped them up, and saw that something was stuck to the underside of the scale into which the goods were tipped for weighing.

'Aha!' said Pink-Whistle to himself 'Oho! So this is another little trick — to stick something heavy under the scale-pan to make goods weigh more than they do! That is how my one and a half pounds of fish seemed to weigh *two* pounds. What horrid cheats!'

Tom Twisty and his wife heard the scales rattling a little and they looked up, wondering if anyone was meddling with them. But there was no one to be seen. Pink-Whistle was quite invisible, of course.

'Funny,' said Twisty to his wife. 'I quite

11

thought I saw that scale-pan move.'

'Nonsense,' said his wife.

Pink-Whistle then took up the weights, and weighed them carefully in his hands. They seemed unusually light to him. Perhaps the Twistys used weights that were too light – so that they did not have to give so many apples, or so much sugar or butter! The cheats!

He took the weights over to another stall, belonging to a man called Bill Bonny. Bill had gone off to his dinner. Pink-Whistle popped one of Bill's pound weights into one side of the scales there, and put Twisty's into the other side. Down went Bill's weight with a bang, and up went Twisty's!

'Oho! So it's what I thought. Twisty is using weights that are much too light. His pound weight is not a pound weight and his half-pound weight only weighs about six ounces instead of eight. The rogue! He must have cheated scores of people all the time he has been here!'

He put back the weights beside Twisty's scales. Twisty heard a little noise and looked up, puzzled. But there was nothing to see, of course. Pink-Whistle looked into the sacks of potatoes. All of them had plenty of dirt as well as potatoes! Every little nasty trick that could be used to cheat people out of their goods was here.

'Time this was put right,' said Pink-Whistle to himself. 'High time! And I'll put it right too. I'll stand by Twisty's stall this afternoon, and give him a shock!'

So that afternoon, when people came to the market once more to buy, Mr Pink-Whistle was standing close to Twisty at his stall. But nobody could see Pink-Whistle. He was still invisible! He was grinning to himself, because he knew he was going to have a good time. So was everyone, except Twisty and his wife.

A little boy came up with a bag. 'Twelve grapefruit, please,' he said.

Twisty beamed all over his nasty face. He took up a grapefruit and tossed it into the bag. 'One – two – three – I say, that was a fine big one, wasn't it – I'll choose you another fat one – here it is – five – and another, six. . . .'

'Hey, you can't count!' boomed a voice right in Twisty's ear, making him jump violently. He wondered which of the crowd round him was shouting like that, and was

13

quite prepared to throw something at him. But he couldn't see anyone shouting.

'Count your grapefruit, sonny,' boomed Mr Pink-Whistle, making Twisty jump again. 'Have you got six?'

'No, five,' said the little boy.

'Story-teller. I gave you six!' shouted Twisty.

'You gave him five!' yelled Pink-Whistle, putting his mouth close to Twisty's ear. 'Begin again! And *I'll* count this time!'

Twisty was scared. He looked round for the man with the fierce voice, but he couldn't see him at all. The little boy tossed the grapefruit on to the stall, grinning. Twisty, looking rather alarmed, began to count again.

'One, two, three' – but a voice boomed in his ear.

'*I'M* COUNTING THIS TIME!' And then the voice went on, as Twisty threw the grapefruit one by one into the boy's bag. 'One, two, three – isn't it a lovely day – three, four, five – you're a nice little boy, you are! Four, five, six, seven – that was a nice fat one, wasn't it – seven, eight, nine, ten – did you say you wanted twelve? Ah, yes, nine, ten, eleven, twelve!'

Of course, you can quite well see that dear old Pink-Whistle was playing Twisty's trick the other way round, giving the little boy far more grapefruit than he asked for, instead of less! Everyone began to shriek with laughter. Twisty was too frightened to say anything, and he meekly let the little boy pay him for twelve

14

grapefruit, when he really had eighteen.

'But I've got eighteen gr . . .' began the little boy in surprise.

'That's all right,' said Mr Pink-Whistle's voice, in Twisty's ear. 'Twisty's pleased about that, aren't you, Twisty?'

Twisty wasn't. But he didn't dare to say so. Then someone went to Mrs Twisty's stall, and asked for twelve pounds of potatoes. Pink-Whistle popped over to her at once.

He watched the masses of dirt going into the scales with the potatoes. Before Mrs Twisty knew what was happening, Pink-Whistle had tipped up the sack and emptied quite half a dozen more pounds into the scales.

'Sorry there's so much dirt,' said Pink-Whistle's booming voice, right in Mrs Twisty's ear. 'You shall have a few extra pounds of potatoes instead. Can't bear to cheat anyone, you know!'

Mrs Twisty jumped. Where *did* that voice come from? And how did the potato sack suddenly tip itself up like that and empty more potatoes into the scales? She began to tremble. All the same, she wasn't going to let so many potatoes go! She picked out about six.

A sharp slap made her drop them into the pan. 'Naughty, naughty!' said the voice. 'Put a few more in for that.'

And to Mrs Twisty's horror, the sack of potatoes appeared to lift itself up and empty another score or so of potatoes into the big scale-pan!

Who had slapped her? She glared round at

15

everyone, but there did not seem to be anyone near enough. All the people were laughing. What a joke! They didn't quite know what was happening, and most of them were feeling very puzzled, but all the same, how they were enjoying themselves! The Twistys were cheats — and now, for the first time, they were being punished well and truly in full view of the market! *What* a joke!

Mrs Twisty said no more about potatoes. She turned away and pretended to be busy. Somebody went up to buy a pound of flour from Twisty. He slapped his pound weight on one side of the scale, and emptied flour into the other.

'*That's* not a pound!' said the Voice, from somewhere near his ear. 'Here, put *this* weight on — it really does weigh a pound!'

And, to Twisty's horror, a pound weight was put into his scales, and his own weighed against it. Everyone cried out in scorn.

'Huh! Look at that! Twisty's weight has gone up and the other has gone down! Twisty's doesn't weigh a pound!'

Twisty began to shake at the knees. 'Good people, it's a mistake,' he stammered. 'There's some trickery going on here....'

'There certainly is,' said the Voice, 'and there has been trickery going on for a long time! Good people, tell Twisty to turn up his scale-pans! See what is underneath!'

Twisty tried to look fierce. He looked round for the man with the voice. Where *could* he be? 'I'll slap your face hard!' cried Twisty, bravely.

'Go on, then!' mocked Pink-Whistle, and poked Twisty in the chest. 'Slap me! Here I am!'

Twisty was terrified. He couldn't bear being punched by someone who wasn't there. The people roared at him.

'Lift up your scale-pans, Mr and Mrs Twisty! Lift up your scale-pans, and let us see underneath!'

Pink-Whistle lifted them up himself, and there, stuck underneath the pans into which goods were put to be weighed, were lumps of clay, flattened on to the pans to make them weigh more than they should.

Then the people went quite mad. They made for the sacks of potatoes and apples, they went for the sacks of flour and bags of pepper, they rushed at the slabs of fish – and before the two bad Twistys knew what was happening, they were being pelted with potatoes, apples and

17

fish, and having flour and pepper emptied all over them!

'You'll be sorry for this,' sobbed Mrs Twisty, 'I'll turn you all out of your houses!'

'WHAT'S THAT?' boomed the Voice that the Twistys now feared more than anything. 'Say that again!'

'No, no!' said Twisty, scared to death. 'She didn't mean it. We're both sorry for all the wrong things we've done. People can help themselves to any of our market goods they please today!'

'And will you behave yourselves in future?' boomed the Voice.

'Yes, yes,' said Twisty. 'Certainly. No doubt about that.'

The Twistys left the market in a hurry, and went home. The people helped themselves to all the goods on the stalls, laughing and chattering. Pink-Whistle laughed too, then made himself visible again and went after the Twistys.

When he got to their house he saw them coming out with their bags. They were off and away! They were too scared to stay in the village of Little-Trees any longer. They caught the first bus that came along, and Mr Pink-Whistle got in with them. The bus would soon pass his own house, so that was very convenient for him.

The Twistys saw the little man opposite them and heard him humming a little tune. Mrs Twisty suddenly noticed his pointed ears, and she nudged her husband.

'Look! That man's half a brownie. Look at his ears. Oh, Twisty — do you think he had anything to do with that upset at the market?'

Pink-Whistle saw them looking at him, and he grinned. Aha! The Twistys wouldn't play such tricks any more! They would be very, very careful in future.

He took out his packet of fish and sniffed at it. Then he looked at Twisty. 'I bought this at the market today,' he said, 'and do you know, though it only weighs a pound and a half, the fellow who sold it to me said it weighed two pounds. And ....'

But the Twistys had leapt out of the bus and gone. They had recognised that Voice. Ooooooh! They were too scared to ride in the bus any longer. Where they went to nobody knows, and certainly nobody cares.

Pink-Whistle chuckled. 'Another thing put right!' he said. 'Won't old Sooty laugh when he hears *this* tale!'

And Sooty certainly did!

2

A wonderful party

Now one day Mr Pink-Whistle met such a nice pair of children that he really had to stop and talk to them. The girl had a bright, smiling face and the boy looked so strong and had such twinkling eyes that Mr Pink-Whistle couldn't help smiling when he saw him.

'Hallo, hallo there!' said Mr Pink-Whistle, looking at the two children. 'Are you twins? You look exactly alike!'

'Yes, we're twins,' said the boy. 'We were born on the same day. Mollie will be eight on Thursday and so shall I.'

'Ha! A birthday!' said Mr Pink-Whistle, who loved presents and surprises. 'I suppose you will be having a party?'

'Oh, of course,' said Mollie. 'Michael has chosen six boys and I have chosen six girls – so it will be a lovely big party; and do you know what Mike and I are going to have – a bran-tub! You see, Grandpa has given us five shillings each for our birthday, and we thought it would be a lovely idea to spend it on presents for our guests.'

'We shall put them in the bran-tub and everyone will draw one out!' said Michael,

doing a little dance of joy on the pavement. 'We're going to buy them now.'

'Dear me, what nice children to think of giving other people presents on their birthday,' thought Mr Pink-Whistle, who loved kind and generous people.

'Mother is making a big birthday cake with both our names on,' said Mollie. 'It's going to have pink icing. She saved up the sugar icing specially for us. And she is making pink, yellow and red jellies, and two big chocolate blancmanges.'

'And we are going to play Blind-Man's Buff and Nuts-in-May, and Postman's Knock, and all kinds of games,' said Mike. 'And there are six boxes of crackers — what do you think of that? Won't everyone enjoy themselves?'

Mr Pink-Whistle walked along with the two happy children and watched them buy twelve lovely presents for their little friends. There was twopence over, and what do you think the children did with it?

'Let's buy twopenny-worth of those pretty pink sweets and give them to this kind little man,' whispered Mollie. 'I do like him!'

So, to Mr Pink-Whistle's great surprise he was given a bag of bright pink sweets by Mollie and Mike!

'Dear me!' he said. 'Dear me — how very sweet and kind of you! Just the sweets I like, too. Thank you very, very much indeed. I do hope you have a wonderful party on Thursday.'

Mr Pink-Whistle whispered magic words to himself when he went out of the shop, and disappeared. He wanted to follow the twins home and find out where they lived. He meant to give them a birthday present each.

So he trotted behind them, although they didn't know it, and saw the house they lived in. He wrote down the name of it in his notebook — Fir-Tree House.

When Thursday came, Mr Pink-Whistle bought two merry birthday cards; a big farmyard for Michael with all kinds of little animals in it; and a doll's house for Mollie, full of the tiniest furniture. Then he set off to Fir-Tree House, hoping that the children would be in so that he could wish them many happy returns of the day.

Their mother came to the door. Mr Pink-

23

Whistle raised his hat politely and asked to see Mollie and Michael.

'Well — have you had whooping-cough?' asked Mrs Brown.

'Er — whooping-cough? What do you mean, exactly?' said Mr Pink-Whistle, very puzzled.

'You see, both the children have got whooping-cough now,' said Mrs Brown. 'The doctor came this morning and said they had caught it. It's such a pity, because it's their birthday, and they are *so* disappointed.'

'Can't they have their party then?' asked Mr Pink-Whistle.

'Oh no,' said Mrs Brown. 'They might give other children their cough. They mustn't have others here for a long time. And, you know, they had got such nice presents for their guests, and I have made a lovely cake and jellies and things. I am really as much disappointed and sad as Mollie and Mike are.'

'Are they in bed?' said Mr Pink-Whistle.

'No,' said Mrs Brown. 'They are not ill, but they just have a nasty cough. They are in the nursery. If you've had whooping-cough, you can go in and see them.'

'Oh, I've had whooping-cough all right,' said Mr Pink-Whistle. 'I had it when I was five. Yes — I'll go and see the children, please.'

So up into the big nursery he went — and, dear me, what sad children he found! Mollie wasn't smiling and Mike had quite lost his twinkle.

'Hallo, hallo!' said Pink-Whistle, bustling in. 'Many happy returns of the day! My, I'm

sorry you've got whooping-cough!'

'It's so dreadfully horrid of it to have happened on our *birthday*!' said Mollie, trying not to cry. 'Why couldn't it have happened tomorrow? We've had our presents and our cards – but we can't have our friends here and let them share our cake and goodies and give them the lovely presents we bought. It doesn't seem fair, does it?'

'It doesn't, and it isn't,' said Mr Pink-Whistle sadly. 'Can't you really have any of your friends to tea?'

'No – because, you see, not one of them has had whooping-cough,' said Mike. 'But perhaps *you* would like to come, if you've had it?'

'Oh, I should. I certainly should,' said Mr Pink-Whistle, beaming. 'And do you know, I believe I could bring some guests who don't mind a scrap about whooping-cough – friends of my own, you know – very jolly ones. Would you like that? Then you could have a party after all.'

'Oooooh – that would be fine,' said the twins, smiling in delight. 'Will you talk to Mother about it?'

So downstairs went Mr Pink-Whistle, leaving the two big parcels he had brought for Mollie and Mike to undo. He told the children's mother what he had said to the children, and she nodded her head.

'I am sure that the friends of a kind little man like you would be nice to have,' she said. 'Bring twelve if you can, because I've got enough food for that number. I'll see you again at four o'clock, I hope.'

Off scurried Mr Pink-Whistle, back to his own little village. He burst in at his own tiny cottage, much to the surprise of Sooty, his big black cat.

'Sooty, Sooty!' cried Mr Pink-Whistle. 'We've got to find twelve people who have had whooping-cough or don't mind about it by four o'clock this afternoon. Will you help me?'

'Well, can't I be one?' asked Sooty at once. 'I don't mind about whooping-cough at all. Would they mind a cat coming?'

'No – I think they'd be pleased,' said Mr Pink-Whistle. 'I'll buy you a new blue party-bow. Now, come on – we must find some more people. What about little Mrs Tickle? She's sweet. And dear Mr Tiddley-Winks –

26

I'm sure the twins would love him and his hat edged with tiddley-winks. Come on, Sooty!'

So off went the two to find more guests for the party. What a surprise for Mollie and Mike when they all arrived!

Now, when four o'clock came, you should have seen the twelve people that went trooping up the garden path of the children's house.

First there was Mr Pink-Whistle himself, of course, beaming all over his plump face, his green eyes shining. Behind him came Sooty, the cat, with a new blue party-bow tied very beautifully.

Then came Mrs Tickle, a darling little person with such tiny feet that when she walked it seemed almost as if she was running by clockwork. There was Mr Tiddley-Winks, a tall thin man whose hat was sewn with red,

green, blue and yellow tiddley-wink counters that jiggled and clattered as he walked.

That was four. The fifth person was the pixie, Tiptoe, who had tucked her wings inside her cloak so that no one in the street should see them. The sixth and seventh guests were two big sandy rabbits, looking rather shy but very pleased, each with a pink bow round his neck.

The eighth guest was a brownie whose beard was so long that he tied it round his waist when he walked, in case he tripped over it. The ninth and tenth were Mr and Mrs Roundy, who were just like their name; and the eleventh and twelfth were two goblin children, all dressed up in their best. They were not very pretty, for their noses turned up and they had such big ears – but they were so smiley that no one could help liking them.

Mrs Brown was most astonished to see such a queer company – especially the cat and the rabbits – but she was too polite to say anything, and helped the goblin children off with their coats.

Well! When Mollie and Michael saw their strange guests trooping into the nursery, they were most excited and pleased. Gracious! What a marvellous party it would be, with rabbits and a cat, and goblin children and a pixie, and the rest.

Everyone had a present to give to Mollie and Michael, of course, though the rabbits only brought a bunch of early primroses each, which they thought were not very good presents – but the twins simply loved the pretty pale-yellow flowers, and Mollie put them into a little blue bowl at once, in the very middle of the birthday table.

You should have seen some of the presents that the guests gave to the children. Mr and Mrs Roundy gave them a dear little mug each, and as soon as it was lifted up to drink from, each mug played a tune. Mollie's played, 'Sing a song of sixpence,' and Mike's played 'Humpty-Dumpty.'

'I shall drink all day long now,' said Mike. 'I think my mug must be magic.'

Mr Tiddley-Winks gave them a set of beautiful tiddley-winks each, of course, and Sooty, the cat, gave them a black china cat exactly like himself – and it mewed when its tail was pulled. So you can guess that it mewed all the afternoon, because somebody or other was always pulling its tail. It really was great fun.

Well, Mrs Brown and the twins soon got used to such strange guests, and the party began. Goodness, it was fun to play nuts-in-May with the rabbits and the cat, and blind-man's buff with Mr Pink-Whistle as the blind man. He kept catching Mrs Roundy, who was a dreadful giggler and could never get out of the way in time.

The tea was gorgeous, because Mrs Tickle had brought along a big tin of her best home-made biscuits, and as they were all made in the shape of toys, with jam right in the middle, they were most exciting.

Mike had a biscuit just like an engine, and

when he squeezed it, the jam came out of the funnel. Everyone thought it was wonderful.

Then they had the bran-tub – and how all the guests loved their presents! Sooty got a clockwork mouse, and when Mike wound it up and set it going Sooty was quite mad with delight, and chased the mouse under chairs and tables till Mrs Brown felt quite giddy to watch him.

'I think this is the finest party anyone ever had,' said Mollie happily. 'Fancy finding twelve guests who don't mind about whooping-cough! I am sorry we couldn't have our proper friends – but I can't help thinking this is a more exciting party with this sort of guest, Mike.'

Mr Pink-Whistle was asked to do a little

magic, because the twins knew now that he was half-magic.

So he was most obliging, and kept appearing and disappearing in a most surprising way. Mollie begged him to whisper the magic words in her ear, so that she could make herself disappear too — but she didn't get them quite right, and to everyone's great astonishment only her legs disappeared.

And there was Mollie running about the room without any legs that could be seen. Mrs Roundy laughed till she cried.

Then they had the crackers. Sooty and the rabbits had never seen crackers before, and when the first one went off BANG, they were dreadfully frightened. Sooty jumped up the chimney at once, and the two rabbits rushed under the sofa.

When Sooty came down at last, he was just as sooty as his name, and Mrs Brown had to hold him under the tap and scrub him clean. Then he sat in front of the fire to be dried, whilst the two rabbits crept out from the sofa and wondered if they dared to pull a cracker themselves.

'Well, let's,' said the bigger rabbit. 'There are caps inside, Whiskers, dear — and you know I've always wanted some sort of hat to wear.'

So they pulled a cracker, and then another, and out came a blue bonnet for Whiskers and a golden crown for Floppy. Goodness, they were pleased!

Then they played tiddley-winks — and you

31

should have seen the way Mr Tiddley-Winks played. He was simply marvellous. He could not only flip counters into the cup – but he could flip just anything.

'Flip this pencil,' said Mike, and Mr Tiddley-Winks flipped it – and it hopped straight into the cup. Then he flipped the poker, and that went into the cup and stood itself quite upright. Then he flipped one of the little dolls out of the dolls' house, and she flipped into the cup and sat there, looking very comfortable.

'You *are* clever,' said Mike. 'I wish I could play tiddley-winks like that.'

Then Mr Pink-Whistle looked at this watch. 'Dear me!' he said. 'We must all go. We have to catch the bus. Good-bye, Mollie dear; good-bye, Mike. We've had a wonderful party, and we thank you very much for such a good time.'

'Thank you for bringing such a lovely lot of guests,' said the twins, and they kissed everyone good-bye – even Sooty, who was terribly proud of being hugged by the two children.

Then they all trooped off to catch a most peculiar yellow-and-purple bus that stopped outside. Mike and Mollie had never seen it before, so they thought it must be a special bus sent to fetch their strange guests. They waved good-bye to them and then looked at one another.

'Dear old Pink-Whistle,' said Mollie. 'Isn't he a darling! He's just the kindest fellow in all the world. When things seemed too horrid for

words, he came along and put everything right.
I wish I was like him.'

'Good-bye, good-bye!' shouted Mike,
waving to Mr Pink-Whistle, who was the last
one to get into the bus. 'Take care of yourself,
Mr Pink-Whistle, and DO come and see us
again!'

Good-bye! Good-bye!

3

A puzzle for the Jones family

One afternoon, when Mr Pink-Whistle was walking down a town street, trying to find a tea-shop where he could have a bun and a cup of coffee, he heard a mew coming from the small front garden of a house.

Mr Pink-Whistle stopped at once. He knew that the mew was from a cat in need of help. Surely it couldn't have been caught in a trap? He opened the gate of the garden and went inside.

A tabby-cat was sitting on the front doorstep of the house mewing pitifully. She was thin and looked very lonely and miserable.

'Poor creature! Won't your family let you in?' said Mr Pink-Whistle. 'I'll ring the bell and tell them. And I'll tell them to give you a good meal, too. You look so thin!'

Mr Pink-Whistle rang the bell loudly. Nobody came to the door. He knocked with the knocker, blim, blam, blim, blam! Nobody came. Then Pink-Whistle saw that the blinds were drawn down, and that the knocker wasn't cleaned, and that an old newspaper lay on the front-door mat.

'Why, they must be away!' he thought. And

just as he thought that, a voice came from over the fence next door.

'Hi! It's no use knocking! The Jones family are away! They've been away two weeks, and are coming back tomorrow.'

'Thank you,' said Pink-Whistle, nodding to the boy who looked over the fence. Then he spoke to the cat. 'And what have you been doing to get yourself so thin and miserable in two weeks, Tabby?'

'Well, my family went without leaving anywhere for me to sleep, and without arranging for any food for me,' said Tabby mournfully. 'I've had hardly anything for my dinner for two weeks, and though I've tried to catch a few mice, it is difficult, because there are hardly any round here. So I've got thin. But what has made me so miserable is that the family I love should treat me like this! It isn't fair.'

'Indeed it isn't!' said Pink-Whistle in a rage. 'What! This horrid family went away and left you all alone and uncared for! I won't have it! I'll go straight to the fish-shop and buy you some fish!'

So off went the angry little man, with the tabby-cat running at his heels, tail well up in the air. Pink-Whistle bought a fine bit of fish and took it back to the cat's garden. The tabby gobbled up the fish, uncooked as it was, and then began to wash itself, looking pleased and happy.

'Now look here, Tabby – I'm going to show that horrid family called Jones what it's like to have no food!' said Mr Pink-Whistle fiercely. 'You just wait till they come home tomorrow. I'll show them! I'll show them!'

The next day was Saturday. The family were coming home after tea, and they had written to ask the milkman to send some milk, the baker to send some bread, the greengrocer to leave some potatoes, the butcher to leave some meat, and the grocer to leave butter, tea, and the rest of the things.

There was a little yard at the back, with a big box in which the tradespeople left their goods if there was no one to take them in at the back door. Each man left his goods in the box and shut down the lid. Mr Pink-Whistle soon found out where the box was, because he made himself invisible and watched where the goods were put.

And then the sly little man opened the lid of the box, took out everything, popped them into an enormous bag he had brought, and ran off down the street. The tabby-cat watched him in amazement.

Pink-Whistle went to a row of poor old tumbledown cottages. In them lived three or four poor families whose children went barefoot. Pink-Whistle had a fine time there. Do you know what he did?

He opened each door of the row of cottages and popped inside the kitchen something that he had taken out of the box in the back-yard! Mrs Tibbles got two loaves of bread. Goodness, wasn't she surprised to see the door open and the loaves hop into the kitchen! She couldn't see Pink-Whistle, of course, because he was quite invisible.

Mrs Harris, next door, was peeling potatoes

at the sink when she saw her door open and a bottle of milk and a large piece of meat come in. She squealed and dropped the potato knife. But she soon got over her fright when she found that the milk and meat stayed on the floor, waiting to be picked up!

Everyone in the row got something. Then Pink-Whistle hurried off to the house again. The Jones family had just come back and were busy unpacking upstairs. The cat was mewing and purring round them, delighted to see the family again, although they had treated her so badly.

It was half-past six. Mrs Jones went out into the yard to fetch in the food, meaning to get Mr Jones, Joan Jones, and John Jones some supper. But there was nothing at all in the box. How angry she was!

She flew upstairs and said that Mr Jones couldn't possibly have posted her cards to the tradesmen, asking them to send the goods. They quarrelled, and then at last John Jones was sent out to see what food he could get before the shops closed.

The dairy was shut, so he could get no milk. The baker had only one stale brown loaf left, and John bought that. He bought a string of sausages, some butter, some bacon and some eggs. Then back he went home.

'Put them in the larder,' called Mrs Jones. 'I'm just coming. Don't leave them on the table or the cat will get them, the greedy thing!'

The cat didn't get them — but someone else did!

Mr Pink-Whistle, quite unseen, slipped into the kitchen and went to the larder. In a trice everything was under his arm, in his big bag! The little man slipped out again — and back to those poor cottages he went, chuckling away to himself.

And what a pleasant surprise the cottagers got again, when eggs, sausages, bread, bacon and butter suddenly appeared round their doors! They couldn't make it out. They ran to the door to see who had put the things there, but they could see no one. Mr Pink-Whistle was invisible. All they heard was a deep chuckle from somewhere near by. It was very puzzling — but very nice!

Well, the Jones family were in a way when they found that the larder was empty. Not a thing was there!

'Did you put the things in the larder as I told you?' asked Mrs Jones. John nodded.

'Of course I did,' he said. 'And shut the door, too. So the cat couldn't have got them.'

'Well, the shops will all be shut now,' said his mother. 'We can't get any food for supper. Your father will have to run round to the dairy early tomorrow morning and get some eggs, milk and butter. We can at least make some sort of breakfast then. And maybe the butcher has some meat over that he can let us have.'

Well, Mr Jones did manage to get some eggs, milk and butter, and a loaf of bread from a neighbour in the morning. He put the loaf on the table, Mrs Jones popped the eggs into a saucepan to boil, put the butter into a dish, and the milk into a jug.

But as soon as she turned her back, the things were gone! Yes – the eggs were whisked out of the saucepan, the loaf disappeared with the butter and milk, and when the Jones family came to breakfast, there wasn't anything for them to have at all! Mr Pink-Whistle had been along again! Only the tabby knew what was happening, for, like most animals, she could see Mr Pink-Whistle, even though he was invisible to human eyes.

There was such a wailing and crying when the children found there was no breakfast. 'We had no supper yesterday – and now no breakfast today!' they wept. 'What is happening? This is simply horrid.'

The butcher let them have some meat although it was Sunday. Mr Jones got a

cabbage from the garden, and Mrs Jones borrowed some flour from a neighbour to make a batter pudding. Everything was put on to cook. The joint sizzled in the oven, and the cabbage boiled in its saucepan. The pudding browned nicely by the meat.

'Goodness! I've never been so hungry in all my life!' said Joan. 'I do hope dinner will be early!'

But gracious me, when Mrs Jones went into the garden for a moment, Pink-Whistle slipped indoors, whipped the meat out of the oven, took the cabbage out of the saucepan, and popped the pudding into a dish he carried. Then off he went again to the row of tumbledown cottages. The people there really thought that they must have gone mad when a

41

large, half-cooked joint appeared, a tender cabbage and a big batter pudding!

But oh, the Jones family! What a way they were in! How they sobbed and cried, all except Mr Jones who wondered what in the world could be happening. The tabby-cat sat and watched them.

'I'm so hungry,' wept Joan. The tabby suddenly got up and went outside. She saw Pink-Whistle sitting on the wall and went up to him.

'Please, Mr Pink-Whistle,' she said, 'don't punish my family any more. I can't bear it. They are all so hungry, and I know what it is to be hungry. I thought I would be pleased when I saw them getting as thin and miserable as I got when they were away. But I find that I am not pleased. I am only sorry.'

'You are a good and kind little cat,' said Pink-Whistle, jumping down from the wall. 'I think you are right. We won't punish them any more. I will get them some food and speak a few words to them.'

Pink-Whistle went to a tea-shop that was open and bought eight penny buns. He took them into the house and put the bag on the table. Everyone was most surprised to see the bag appear out of the air, because they couldn't see Pink-Whistle, of course.

'Look – what is it – how did it come – oh, who put that bag there?' cried the Jones family.

'I did!' said Pink-Whistle, making his voice very deep and solemn. 'I am Pink-Whistle,

your cat's good friend. You left her without
food for two weeks — so I took away *your* food
to make you feel what it was like to be hungry
and not to have anything to eat. But your cat is
sorry for you, and so I will not punish you any
more. I have brought you something to eat.
Look after your cat in future, or you will be
VERY SORRY!'

There was a silence after this speech. It
seemed to come out of the air, and was very
strange to the Jones family. They stood or sat,
their eyes wide open, wondering who was
speaking. Then they opened the bag. There
were only eight penny buns there — but, dear
me, how pleased everyone was to see them!

And you will be glad to know that each of
the Jones family felt ashamed of having left
their poor cat without food or sleeping-place,
and they gave her a bit of their buns. She is
happy now, and always on the lookout for her
good friend, Mr Pink-Whistle. When she sees
him coming she runs up to his legs, rubs
against them, and purrs. And if he is invisible,
it *does* look funny to *see* Tabby rubbing herself
against nothing! You would laugh if you saw
her!

4

Mr Pink-Whistle and the balloon

There was once a little girl who loved balloons
very much indeed. Her name was Susie, and
whenever she went to a party, which was about
once a year, she always hoped that she would
be given a balloon, and sometimes she got her
wish.

Now Susie very badly wanted a blue
balloon. She had had a red one, and a yellow
one, and a green one — but she had never had a
blue one.

'I think blue balloons are the prettiest of all,'
said Susie. 'I wish I could have a blue balloon
on a long piece of string. I'd show it to all the
other children.'

Now one day a balloon-woman came to
Susie's village. She was rather like a balloon
herself, for she was round and fat, and her red
shawl shone brightly. She carried behind her a
great bunch of balloons to sell to the children.
They were the biggest and most beautiful that
the boys and girls had ever seen.

Susie ran to look at them. The balloon-
woman had a little stool with her, and she sat
down on this at a corner. 'Buy a balloon!' she
kept shouting. 'Buy a balloon!'

44

'How much are they?' asked Susie. 'I've a penny at home.'

'What, a penny for beautiful big balloons like these!' cried the balloon-woman. 'No, no – these are threepence each, and well worth it, too.'

'Oh – threepence!' said Susie, disappointed. 'That's very dear. But oh, look at that lovely blue one there! How I would like to have it!'

She stared at the blue balloon. It really was the biggest of the bunch, and it bobbed up and down as the breeze took it. Susie felt that she simply must have it.

'I must earn some money!' she thought. 'If only I could get another two pennies. Then with my own penny I should have threepence, and that would be enough.'

She walked down the road, thinking hard.

She passed Mrs Jones in her garden, and Mrs Jones called out to her.

'Susie! Whatever are you thinking about? You do look so solemn!'

'I'm thinking how I could earn two pennies,' said Susie. 'It's very difficult. I do so want to buy a blue balloon.'

'Well, now I want a little job doing,' said Mrs Jones, 'and I'm willing to give a penny for it. I want a parcel taken down to the post office.'

'Oh, I can do that for you,' said Susie.

'It's a heavy parcel, and the post office is a long way off,' said Mrs Jones. 'You'd better see the parcel before you decide. I wanted my Jack

to take it for me, but he's had to go to bed with a bad cold, and I can't leave him and take it myself.'

Mrs Jones showed Susie the parcel. It certainly was rather large. 'But I can carry it all right,' said Susie, 'and I do so badly want the balloon that I'd be glad to take an even heavier parcel for you!'

The little girl set off to the post office. The parcel certainly was heavy! It made her arms ache before she had gone very far. In fact, by the time she had almost reached the post office, she had to stop and rest. She put the parcel down on a little wall, and hung her tired arms down.

And it was there that our old friend, kind Mr Pink-Whistle, met her. He was coming up the street, looking about him as usual, when he saw Susie.

'Hallo, little girl!' he said. 'That seems a very heavy parcel to carry!'

'Well, it is rather,' said Susie. 'My arms ache a lot. But I'm having a rest now.'

'Let me carry it the rest of the way for you,' said Mr Pink-Whistle.

'No, thank you,' said Susie. 'You see, I am earning a penny for taking it to the post office, and if you carried it for me, it wouldn't be quite fair to get the penny.'

'I see,' said Mr Pink-Whistle. 'I am very pleased to meet a child who knows what is fair and what is not. Do you want the penny for anything special?'

'I do, rather,' said Susie. 'Have you seen the balloon-woman at the corner? Well, she has a most beautiful big blue balloon, and I am longing to buy it. I have never in my life had a blue balloon, you know. It costs threepence, and I am earning a penny towards it. I have a penny already, and when I earn another penny then I can buy the blue balloon.'

The little girl picked up the parcel and went on again, smiling at Mr Pink-Whistle. He went on his way, too, hoping that Susie would be able to buy what she wanted.

Susie was tired when she got back to Mrs Jones. She was pleased to have a nice bright penny. She put it into her pocket and ran home.

She told her mother about the penny, and how much she wanted to earn another penny to buy the balloon.

'Well, Susie dear,' said Mother, 'if you want

to earn a penny, you can turn out the hall cupboard, and put it tidy for me.'

Susie didn't like turning out cupboards, because spiders sometimes lived in cupboards, and she was afraid of them. Still, it would be lovely to earn the last penny towards the blue balloon!

So off she went to the hall cupboard with a duster, a dustpan and a brush. She emptied out all the boots and shoes, bats and balls, and the things that usually live in hall cupboards, and then she swept the cupboard out well, and dusted it round. She put back all the things very neatly and tidily, felt glad there had been no spider, and called to her mother to come and see if she had done her job properly.

'That's very nice, Susie,' said Mother. 'Here is your penny. Now you can go and buy your blue balloon!'

Susie was excited. She took the two pennies she had and the penny Mrs Jones had given her, and off she went to the balloon-woman. The big blue balloon was still there, floating at the top of the bunch! Lovely!

Susie gave the woman her three pennies, and went off with the glorious blue balloon. It really was very big indeed, and was exactly the colour of the sky in April, so you can guess what a pretty blue it was.

And just as she got round the corner, who should come along but Big Jim! Big Jim was a horrid boy, who loved to tease all the little children. Susie was afraid of him, because Big Jim often pulled her hair and pinched her.

She turned back, but Big Jim had seen her. He came running after her.

'Let's have a look at your balloon!' he shouted. 'Let me hold the string.'

Now Susie knew quite well that if she let Big Jim hold the string, he would go off with her lovely balloon and she would never see it again. So she held it very tightly, and shook her curly head.

'If you don't let me hold your balloon I'll burst it!' cried Big Jim. 'Look – see this pin? Well, I'll stick it right into your balloon if you won't let me hold it!'

Susie held the string fast and began to run down the road. Big Jim ran after her and caught her. He made a jab at the balloon with the pin.

POP!

The balloon burst! Susie stared in horror. Instead of a marvellous blue balloon bobbing in the air there was now only a ragged bit of blue rubber on the ground. Susie burst into loud sobs. How she sobbed.

It is always a dreadful shock to any child when a balloon goes pop, but it was extra dreadful to Susie, because she had worked so hard to get the money for it. Big Jim gave a loud laugh and ran off. He thought he had played a fine joke on Susie.

Susie sobbed and sobbed. She really felt as if her heart was broken. She didn't hear footsteps coming up close to her – but she suddenly felt an arm round her shoulder.

'What's the matter, my dear?' said a kind voice – and, lo and behold, it was Mr Pink-Whistle again! He had heard the sound of crying, and come along to see what was the matter.

'Oh, it's my beautiful blue balloon!' wept Susie. 'Big Jim burst it with a pin because I wouldn't let him hold it. And I worked so hard to get two pennies to buy it. And now it's gone. And the balloon-woman hasn't another blue balloon at all. It was the only one.'

'It's a shame!' said Mr Pink-Whistle fiercely. 'It's not fair! I won't have it! Where does Big Jim live?'

'At the first house round the corner,' wept Susie. 'But even if you go and scold him, it won't bring back my balloon, will it?'

'You go home and cheer up,' said Mr Pink-Whistle. 'I'll be along this evening with a
50

surprise. Now, dry your eyes and smile. That's better! Good-bye!"

And off went Mr Pink-Whistle to Big Jim's. My, what a surprise was coming to that bad boy!

Mr Pink-Whistle looked very angry as he marched down the street. He turned the corner, and came to the first house there. That was where Big Jim lived. Mr Pink-Whistle looked over the hedge.

He could hear a boy whistling in one of the rooms upstairs. That must be Big Jim. Pink-Whistle muttered a few strange words to himself – and in a trice he had disappeared! He was still there, of course, but nobody could see him except any of the fairy-folk.

Pink-Whistle went round the back way. The kitchen door was open, and he slipped inside. The cook was there, doing some washing-up, but she didn't see Pink-Whistle, of course. He went into the hall and up the stairs, frightening the cat who had no idea that anybody was there – and yet she could hear footsteps!

Big Jim was in his bedroom, putting six big beautiful glass marbles away in their box. He was very proud indeed of those marbles. They were the nicest in the town, and all the boys at Jim's school loved them and wished they were theirs. But Jim was not going to give any away! Not he!

'Are you the bad boy that burst Susie's balloon?' asked Pink-Whistle in a deep voice just near to Big Jim's ear. The boy nearly jumped out of his skin.

'Oooooh!' he said in a fright, looking all round. But, of course, he could see no one at all.

'Did you hear what I SAID?' boomed Pink-Whistle. 'I said, "Are you the bad boy that burst Susie's balloon?"'

'I – I – I – did burst a b-b-b-b-balloon,' stammered Big Jim in a fright. 'It was an accident.'

'That's not the TRUTH!' said Pink-Whistle angrily. 'You did it on purpose.'

'Who are you?' asked Big Jim. 'And where are you? I can't see anybody. I'm frightened.'

'Good!' said Pink-Whistle. 'Very good. You deserve to be frightened. Now – I'm going to make blue balloons out of something belonging to you! What have you got to give me?'

'Nothing,' said Big Jim. 'I haven't any balloons – or anything in the least like balloons.'

'What were those things you were putting into a box?' asked Pink-Whistle, and he opened the lid of the marble-box. Inside lay the greeny-bluey-yellow glass marbles, winking and blinking in their box. 'Ah – marbles! These will do nicely. You shall give me these.'

'Indeed I shan't!' said Big Jim, snatching the box away as it rose into the air, lifted by Pink-Whistle's invisible hand. 'Nobody shall have those. They are my own special best marbles, the finest in the town! Put them down!'

Well, Pink-Whistle was not going to be spoken to like that! He rapped his hand smartly on to Jim's, and the boy gave a yell and dropped the box of marbles. They rolled all over the floor.

'Pick them up and give them to me,' ordered Pink-Whistle. Jim wouldn't. He just stood there, sulking to see his precious marbles scattered over the floor. And then suddenly an invisible hand did to him what he had often done to smaller boys and girls. His hair was sharply pulled!

'Ow!' said Big Jim. 'Don't! Oh, if only I could get hold of you! Wouldn't I pull *your* hair!'

'Pick up those marbles!' ordered Pink-Whistle again, and his voice was so cold and angry that Big Jim found himself bending down and picking them all up. He put them back into the box.

Pink-Whistle, still invisible, took a piece of

chalk from his pocket and drew a little circle on the floor. He put one of the marbles into it.

Then he muttered some words that sounded rather queer and frightening to Jim, and emptied a little blue powder over the big glass marble.

'Now, blow hard on your marble until I tell you to stop,' commanded Pink-Whistle. 'Go on. Kneel down and blow. Quick!'

Big Jim was so afraid of having his hair pulled again that he did as he was told. He knelt down and blew on the marble – and a very strange and peculiar thing happened! It began to blow up, just as a balloon does when breath is blown into it! It changed from a round glass marble with yellow and green streaks in it, to a fine big yellow-green balloon. Marvellous!

'Oooh, that's funny,' said Big Jim. 'My glass marble has changed into a balloon. I shall like taking that about with me.

'It's not for you,' said Pink-Whistle, taking the balloon out of the circle and quickly tying a piece of string on to it. 'It's for Susie. Now here's the next one. Blue, please!'

Mr Pink-Whistle put a blue-green marble into the circle of chalk and once again Big Jim had to blow. How he blew! He didn't want to, but he was really afraid of the person he couldn't see but could only hear and feel!

That marble blew up into a balloon too – a fine bluey-green one that Pink-Whistle quickly tied up with another piece of string.

Then into the circle went the third marble.

'Oh, I say,' said Big Jim. 'I'm not going to have any more of my beautiful glass marbles changed into balloons. I just won't have it!'

A hard hand came out and caught hold of Jim's right ear, just in the same way that Jim had so often taken hold of other people's ears! His head was pulled towards the circle, and he had to blow! He blew and he blew. That marble was very hard to blow up, but Pink-Whistle didn't leave go his hold on Jim's ear until the balloon was really quite enormous.

Well, Big Jim had to blow all his precious marbles into balloons! Soon there were six fine balloons waving in the bedroom on the end of strings – and the box of marbles was empty!

'Thank you,' said Pink-Whistle, taking all the strings into one hand, 'Susie shall have all these. I am sure she will especially love this big

blue one made out of your best blue marble, because it is almost exactly the colour of the one you burst. Well, good-bye.'

'Don't take those balloons to Susie,' said Big Jim with tears in his eyes. 'You know quite well they are really my marbles that you've changed by some magic. Please, please, don't take them.'

'How many times have children said, "Please, please," to you, Big Jim, when you have been unkind to them?' asked Pink-Whistle. 'Did you take any notice? No, you didn't. Well, neither shall I. You needed a lesson, my boy, and you've had it. Learn from it and it won't be wasted. You have had to give up something you really loved yourself in order to make up for robbing someone else of something they loved. Remember what it feels like, and be kinder in future!'

Off went the little brownie-man, taking the string of balloons with him. He met Jim's mother in the hall, and she was most amazed and astonished to see a string of balloons going through the hall by themselves — for she couldn't see anyone holding them, of course!

'Pardon me, Madam!' said Pink-Whistle politely, forgetting that he was invisible.

'Oh! Gracious me — talking balloons!' cried Jim's mother, and fled into the kitchen. Pink-Whistle chuckled, and went out of the front door. He trotted along to Susie, first making himself seen, because he knew that people would be most astonished to see balloons floating down the street by themselves.

He came to Susie's house. Susie was in the front garden. Her eyes were red, and she looked sad. When she saw Pink-Whistle coming along with a whole bunch of balloons, she gave a squeal of delight.

'Oh! What marvellous balloons! Oh, where did you get that wonderful blue one from? It's even bigger than the one Big Jim burst!'

'I got these from Big Jim,' said Pink-Whistle. 'I made them from his precious marbles! They are stronger than ordinary balloons, my dear. Take them and enjoy them!'

Susie took the strings, going red with surprise and delight. 'Oh!' she said, 'I shall give a tea-party, and let each of my guests have a balloon to take home.'

'Well, the big blue one is especially yours,' said Pink-Whistle. 'Be sure you keep that!'

So Susie did, of course, and she still has it hanging in her bedroom. She gave the others away at a party, and how the children loved them! Wouldn't it be nice if Pink-Whistle came along when any of *our* balloons went POP? Well – you never know!

5

Mr Pink-Whistle's circus

There was once a little girl called Eileen, who was feeling very excited because she had been asked to go to the circus.

Her friend was going with her mother, and they asked Eileen to go, too. So she was very happy, and she counted the days till the Great Day came.

'Mother, it's Galliano's Circus,' she said happily. 'I shall see Lotta on her horse, Black Beauty, and I shall see Jimmy and his performing dog, Lucky. I shall see Jumbo, the dear old elephant, playing cricket with his keeper, and I shall see Lilliput and all his monkeys. Oh, won't it be fun?'

The day came at last. Eileen woke up – but oh, what a pity, she had a horrid sore feeling in her throat that made her choke and cough. Mother heard her and came in.

'Have you got a sore throat?' she asked Eileen. The little girl didn't want to say yes, because she knew that sore throats meant being kept in bed – but she always told her mother the truth, so she nodded her head.

'It's not very bad, Mother,' she said. 'It won't stop my going to the circus. I can hardly feel it.'

Then she coughed again, and that hurt her throat. Mother made her open her mouth.

'Oh, darling,' she said, 'you really have got a very nasty throat. I simply daren't let you go out today. And, besides, Mary might catch it if you go with her. You can't possibly go out — you must stay in bed.'

Poor Eileen. She began to cry bitterly, and buried her face in her pillow. 'It's not fair,' she wept. 'Just the very day I was going to the circus — the VERY day! Oh, I do feel so unhappy. Now Mary will go without me. They will take someone else. Somebody else will have my treat. Mother, it's NOT FAIR.'

'No — it doesn't seem fair, darling,' said Mother. 'But things aren't always fair, you know. Cheer up. I will go out and buy you a toy this afternoon when you sleep. Then you shall have it at tea-time.'

Mother went out of the room. Eileen cried for a little while, then she fell asleep. She didn't want any breakfast, and she didn't want any dinner. Her throat hurt her. She was cross and miserable. When Mother tucked her up for an afternoon rest, Eileen began to sob again.

'Mary and her mother are just starting out for the circus. They're catching the bus. Mother, it isn't fair!'

'Now don't cry any more or you won't sleep,' said Mother, and she went to the door. 'I'm just going out to buy you a surprise.'

Eileen heard the front door bang. She tried to go to sleep, but she couldn't. She kept thinking of Mary. Now they would have arrived at the circus. Now they would be taking their seats round the ring. Now the band would play.

She began to cry again. She wasn't really a cry-baby, but when you feel ill you can't help crying at all kinds of things, can you?

'I don't think it's a bit fair,' wept the little girl. 'I don't, I don't.'

Now who should come along under the window at that very minute but dear old Mr Pink-Whistle! You know how he loves to put things right, if he can – so you can guess that he stopped at once and listened.

'A little girl in trouble!' he said to himself. 'I must look into this!'

He went to the front door and pushed it. It opened to him, for he was half-magic. Up the stairs he went and into Eileen's room. The little girl heard him opening the door, and she stared
60

at him in surprise, for he had the green eyes
and pointed ears of the fairy-folk.

'Hallo,' said Mr Pink-Whistle. 'What's the
trouble?'

'I was going to the circus today – but now
I've got a bad throat and I can't,' said Eileen,
the tears running down her cheeks again. 'Who
are you? I like you.'

'I'm Mr Pink-Whistle,' said the little man. 'I
like you, too. I think you would be quite pretty
if you didn't spoil your face with crying.'

'Well, you'd cry, too, if you couldn't go to
the circus after all,' said Eileen. 'I just simply
can't help it. I keep thinking of it.'

'I suppose you wouldn't like to see my
circus, would you?' suddenly asked Mr Pink-
Whistle. 'I mean I'm sure it isn't as good as
Galliano's – but it's quite fun.'

'But how can I see it if I'm in bed?' said Eileen in astonishment.

'Easily!' said Pink-Whistle. 'There's room on your bed for my circus to perform. Do you mind putting your legs down flat? That's right. Now look – this is the ring – and you are the people looking on, so you must clap when anything good is done.'

'But where's the circus?' asked Eileen.

'Just a minute, just a minute,' said Mr Pink-Whistle, and he ran into the room next door, which was Eileen's nursery. There were plenty of toys there and it didn't take Pink-Whistle long to rub a little magic on to the ones he wanted for his circus! His magic made them all come alive, and in half a minute he had told them all what to do. Then he went back into the bedroom.

'The circus is coming!' he said. 'Listen to the band!'

In came the band! It was the baby doll carrying the musical box, playing a merry tune by turning the handle round and round – and the pink cat playing the little drum in time to the tune – rum-ti-tum-ti-tum, tum-ti-tum-ti-tum! They climbed up on to the bed and settled down to play their little band together. Eileen was so surprised!

Then in came the toy elephant, Jumbo, led by his keeper, one of the boy-dolls! They climbed up on to the bed, too, and to Eileen's great joy they played cricket together just like the real Jumbo and his keeper at the big circus. Her toy elephant was very clever at hitting the

62

ball that the doll threw to him, and once he hit it so hard that it bounced on Mr Pink-Whistle's nose with a loud 'ping'!

That made everyone laugh. Eileen clapped loudly. 'Now come the next performers,' said Pink-Whistle. The band struck up a merry tune again, and rum-ti-tum-ti-tum went the drum. In came the sailor doll with all the teddy bears tied together in a row.

'The performing bears!' said Pink-Whistle. 'Play up, band — the bears want to dance!'

Well, those teddy bears did dance! They danced all over the bed, they rolled about, they grunted and growled, and they had just as good a time as Eileen herself had.

'Well, I'd no idea my bears could be so funny, Mr Pink-Whistle!' she said. 'If I laugh much more I'll get a stitch in my side.'

Then in galloped the little brown horse without the wooden cart it usually pulled along. Riding on its back was the fairy doll! She did look simply lovely, and Eileen was most surprised to see how clever she was! She stood up on the horse's back, and galloped over the bed like that. Then she stood on one leg only and didn't fall off once.

'Marvellous!' said Eileen. 'Oh, Mr Pink-Whistle, this is simply lovely. What's next?'

'Your two monkeys come next,' said the little man. 'Here they are.'

And in they came, grinning all over their faces. What a time they had! They didn't stay on the bed. They leapt all over the room, and swung by their tails from the lamp that hung

63

down from the ceiling. They climbed all over Pink-Whistle, and when he took some bananas from his pocket and gave them to the monkeys, they peeled them neatly and gobbled them up.

'Aren't they clever?' said Eileen. 'Oh, Mr Pink-Whistle, I think I'd rather see your circus than even Mr Galliano's — because, you see, your circus is made of all my own toys, and I really didn't know they were so clever. Oh, look — here come all my toy soldiers on horseback!'

The soldiers galloped in. The band struck up again — and hey presto, all those horses began to dance prettily round the bed in time to the music — just like the horses do in any circus. It was marvellous to watch. Suddenly the front door opened. It was Mother back from her walk. Eileen stared at Mr Pink-Whistle.

'That's Mother!' she said. 'I wonder what she's brought me. Oh, Mr Pink-Whistle, do stay and let her see the circus, too.'

'Sorry, little girl, I can't,' said Pink-Whistle. 'I don't want your mother to see me. I'm going to disappear and slip down the stairs. Watch me!'

Eileen watched him — and to her very great amazement the merry little man seemed to dissolve like sugar in a cup — and then he wasn't there at all! But his voice came to her from near the door.

'Good-bye. So glad you liked my circus. Do things seem a bit fairer now?'

'Oh yes!' cried Eileen. And then down the

stairs went Pink-Whistle, opened the front door, and was gone. Mother saw the front door opening and shutting by itself and she was most surprised. You see, she couldn't see Pink-Whistle at all.

She went up the stairs – and as soon as she came to Eileen's door, an extraordinary thing happened. All the toys had hopped down from Eileen's bed and were running back to the nursery. There they went – monkeys, dolls, bears, and all. Mother simply couldn't believe her eyes.

'I must be imagining things,' she thought. She peeped into the nursery. All the toys were in their places, as still as could be. Nobody could ever imagine they had been in Mr Pink-Whistle's circus all afternoon. 'Eileen! What do you think I've bought you?' cried Mother, going into the bedroom. 'Look – a little toy circus! Won't you love that?'

'Yes, I will,' said Eileen, sitting up joyfully. 'But, Mother – I shall always like Mr Pink-Whistle's circus the very best of all!'

And I'm sure I would, too, wouldn't you?

6

Mr Pink-Whistle and the cowards

Paul went to school every morning, feeling afraid. He wasn't afraid of school, or of his teacher, or of any of his lessons. He was afraid of two boys who went to the same school as he did.

Every morning these two boys lay in wait for Paul. He had to go down their lane, and sometimes they hid behind the big oak tree to jump out at him, and sometimes they hid behind the hedge. He never knew where they would be.

They never hurt him. They didn't kick or pinch or punch – they teased Paul in another way.

They threw his school cap over the hedge or up into a tree. They threw his school bag into the pond. They would take his lunch and scatter it over the grass. And Paul couldn't possibly stop them.

'You are cowards,' he once said to John and Alan. 'You wouldn't do this to me if there was only one of you, because I could fight you then. But I can't fight two of you. I shall report you to our teacher if you do this any more.'

'Well, if you tell tales, we'll tease you all the more,' said Alan.

'We might even take off your shoes and stockings and put them on the old goat over there,' said John.

Well, Paul knew quite well that they were likely to do what they said, for they didn't seem to care a bit what they did. So he didn't tell. He didn't like telling tales anyway, but he became very miserable about his teasing, because he got into trouble at home and at school over his lost caps, his wet school-bag and books, and his excuses over his lost lunch.

'Surely there must be times when it's best to tell tales?' he thought to himself. 'Why should I keep getting into trouble like this for things that are not my fault? Still – I should get into worse trouble from John and Alan if they knew I'd told tales – they might begin to pinch and kick me. I'm too small to fight both of them at once.'

Well, things went on like this all through the summer term. Poor Paul had to have two new caps, because John threw one of his into the middle of a gorse bush far too prickly to rescue it from, and then Alan threw the second cap up a telegraph post and it hung there on the top of the post, impossible to reach.

Twice Paul was scolded and punished for bringing school books soaking wet to school. But how could he help it? John had again thrown his bag into the pond, scaring all the ducks, and soaking everything inside the bag.

And then one day something happened. Paul was going along to school, a little earlier than usual, hoping to slip down the lane before

John and Alan came along. And up the lane
came a funny little man, whose pointed ears
showed that he was half a brownie.

It was Mr Pink-Whistle, of course, but
nobody could know it because he couldn't
be seen. He was invisible, but he had quite
forgotten that, and was stamping along gaily,
whistling loudly.

Now, half-way down the lane John and
Alan were hiding behind a tree, waiting for
Paul, and when they heard the footsteps and
the whistling they felt sure it was Paul coming
along as usual. So, to Mr Pink-Whistle's
enormous astonishment, the boys suddenly
leapt out as he came by, shouting fiercely, their
arms outstretched to catch Paul. But Paul
wasn't there – no one was there! They couldn't
see Pink-Whistle – and they couldn't hear him
either, now, for he had stopped walking in
amazement and was no longer whistling.

'Well!' said John, in astonishment. 'I thought I heard Paul. But there's no one here!'

'I heard steps and whistling,' said Alan. 'Oh, look – there's Paul – coming down the lane. Come on, let's give his mac to the old goat to eat! Before Paul can get it away from him, he'll have munched big holes in it!'

Mr Pink-Whistle listened to all this in the greatest surprise. Give a mackintosh to a goat to eat? These boys must be mad!

John and Alan pounced on poor Paul. They dragged his dark blue mac off his arm. 'The old goat wants it for his dinner!' said Alan, with a grin.

'No, don't' said Paul, in alarm. 'My mother has just paid a lot of money for that mac. It's new. Don't be so mean.'

But the mac was wrenched away and thrown over the hedge for the goat to eat. Paul was left to try and get it back whilst the other boys ran off to school, laughing.

'Beasts!' said Paul, climbing over the hedge to get his mac. The goat had already bitten off a button. 'Why don't they leave me alone? They throw my caps away, they throw my bag into the pond, they spoil everything of mine that they can. And I can't stop them! Nobody can!'

'Excuse me – but I think I can do something about it,' said Mr Pink-Whistle, appearing so suddenly that both Paul and the goat jumped in surprise. The goat dropped the mac and ran away. Paul stood and stared at Pink-Whistle in amazement.

'Where did you come from?' he asked. 'You suddenly appeared!'

'Yes. I forgot I was invisible,' said Pink-Whistle. 'I didn't mean to give you quite such a shock. Let me have a look at that mac.'

There was a big tear in it and a button was gone. It was in the goat, so there was no getting that back. But somehow Pink-Whistle managed to mend the mac. A new button seemed to grow in the right place, and the big tear pressed its edges together, gave a peculiar kind of squeak and disappeared.

'I say,' said Paul, half-scared. 'I say – you're a bit magic, aren't you?'

'Just a bit,' said Pink-Whistle. 'Now – you'd better rush off to school, or you'll be late. Leave things to me. I have a feeling I'm going to interfere a little. If you want to see a bit of fun, hide behind that tree at the end of the morning.'

Paul stared hard at Pink-Whistle. He couldn't make him out. He liked the little man very much indeed, and he thought he had the brightest twinkle in his eyes that he had ever seen. He nodded, put his mac over his arm, and sped off to school, wondering what was going to happen.

At the end of the morning Paul shot off before John and Alan left. Now it was his turn to hide behind the tree – not to pounce out, but to watch. He couldn't see Mr Pink-Whistle anywhere. He wondered if he could have imagined him.

But Pink-Whistle was there all right. He had

made himself invisible again, that was all. He waited for John and Alan, and very soon along they came, kicking a stone between them.

'Excuse me,' said Pink-Whistle, in a loud but polite voice. The boys stopped in surprise. They could see no one.

'I want to borrow your caps,' said Pink-Whistle, still very polite. To the two boys' dismay their caps suddenly whisked off their heads, flew up into the air and landed on the exact tops of two chimneys belonging to a nearby cottage.

'And now your shoes, please,' said Pink-Whistle, and their laces were undone, and their shoes pulled off, before they knew what was happening!

Up into the air went the four shoes. Two landed on the old billy-goat's horns and two on the horns of a most astonished cow. Neither of the boys dared go and get them. The cow looked angry and the goat knew how to butt very hard.

'Fine,' said Pink-Whistle, who still couldn't be seen. 'So kind of you to let me have your things. But still, why not? You take Paul's things, don't you? So, of course, you are willing to lend me yours.'

'Who's speaking? Who's doing all this?' said John, clutching Alan's arm.

Behind the tree there sounded a chuckle. It came from Paul, who was really enjoying himself. Now Alan and John knew what it was like to be teased and not be able to stop the teaser!

Mr Pink-Whistle hadn't nearly finished. No, when he did a thing he did it really thoroughly!

He stripped off the boys' stockings next, made the billy-goat stand still, and then slipped them on to each leg. The goat was rather pleased. The stockings were warm, he felt grand in them, and he could always eat them when he was tired of them. He trotted round the field in them, looking rather peculiar because he still had a pair of shoes on his horns.

Alan and John were very scared by now, and began to run away. But a strong and firm hand took hold of each of them.

'No, don't go. I would like to borrow your school-bags, please.'

So off came their school satchels. One sailed away to the top of a tall chestnut tree, and the other fell into the stream and sailed down it merrily, with pens, pencils, and papers leaking out of it. Oh dear, now they couldn't do their homework, and the teacher would be very angry!

Their ties came off next, flew up towards the telegraph wires and then tied themselves round a wire in neat bows. It was really most extraordinary. Even Paul forgot to laugh for a moment, and felt a bit scared. This little invisible man must know a lot of magic!

'Don't!' begged Alan, in alarm, holding on to his coat and shorts, afraid that they would go next. 'Don't! Who are you, doing this? Don't do any more!'

Mr Pink-Whistle hadn't quite finished. He

pulled out the boys' handkerchiefs, threw them into the field, and the goat at once ate them both. He didn't really mind what he ate. He had once tried to eat a tin and many times he had eaten newspapers, rope, paper-bags, and cardboard cartons. So he was quite pleased with the handkerchiefs.

'Well, thank you very much,' said Mr Pink-Whistle politely. 'That's all for this morning. I'll meet you here again another day perhaps. That would be very nice.'

'No, oh no!' cried Alan and John, and fled down the lane in their bare feet as fast as they could go. Paul came out from behind the tree, laughing.

'I don't know quite where you are,' he said to Mr Pink-Whistle, who was still invisible, 'but thank you very much for interfering. Oh dear, look at those caps on the chimneys still.'

Pink-Whistle suddenly appeared, looking

very pleased with himself. 'Yes, they look comic up there, don't they?' he said. 'I did enjoy myself. Well, my boy, I have a feeling that those two boys won't tease you much more. I don't believe they liked my bit of interference! I'll be along here again for the next few days, so call out if you want me.'

But Paul didn't call out, because John and Alan never went down that lane again. They were so afraid of meeting the polite and powerful little invisible man that they went another way to school. It took them twice as long, so they had to start much earlier. Paul never had any bother with them again.

The funny thing is the school ties are still tied in bows round the telegraph wire. Nobody can imagine who put them there – but if you see them you'll know. It was all because Mr Pink-Whistle interfered!

7

Mr Pink-Whistle is rather funny

Once when Mr Pink-Whistle was walking down a rather lonely road he met a small boy who was crying bitterly.

Pink-Whistle could never bear to see anyone unhappy, and stopped at once.

'What's the matter?' he said. 'You tell me what's the matter, and maybe I can put it right.'

'My mother s-s-sent me to buy some b-b-bread,' wept the small boy, 'and the boy who lives round the corner took the money from me and ran off with it. And my mother will s-s-s-spank me.'

'Dear, dear!' said Pink-Whistle. 'I'm very sorry to hear that. Come with me, and we'll buy the bread together. Then maybe if we meet this bad boy you can point him out to me.'

So they went to the baker's shop together and bought some bread. Pink-Whistle paid for it, and they went out in the street again.

But the bad boy was nowhere to be seen. So Pink-Whistle said good-bye and sent the small boy home.

He set off down the road again, a little plump man with the pointed ears of a brownie, and a merry, twinkling look in his eyes. But soon he heard the sound of sobbing again, and he saw two little girls running on the opposite side of the road, tears pouring down their red cheeks.

'Dear, dear me!' said Pink-Whistle to himself. 'All the children seem to be in tears today!'

He ran across and stopped the two little girls. They hadn't any hankies, so he dried their tears with his great big one.

'Now, you tell me what's wrong,' he said.

'Well, we were going to the sweet-shop to buy some chocolate,' said one of the little girls, 'and a horrid boy came up to us and asked us where we were going. And when we told him we were going to the sweet shop he said how much money had we?'

'And when we showed him, he snatched it out of our hands and ran away,' wept the other

little girl. 'So we can't buy our chocolate, and we saved up a whole week for it.'

'Well, well,' said Pink-Whistle, holding out his hand. 'Come along and we'll go and buy some. I don't think that bad boy will stop you if you are with *me*.'

So they all went to the sweet-shop, and Pink-Whistle bought plenty of chocolate for the two little girls. They beamed at him.

'Oh, thank you! You *are* kind!' they said. 'We do hope we shan't meet that big boy and have him take our chocolate from us!'

'I'll see you right home,' said Pink-Whistle. So off they went, and he saw them safely home. But they didn't meet the bad boy as Pink-Whistle had hoped they would.

Now, just after he had left them, what should he hear but yet another child crying. Surely it couldn't be someone that bad boy had robbed again? Mr Pink-Whistle hurried round the corner to see.

A very small girl was there, holding the corner of her dress to her eyes. 'He took the sausages!' she wept. 'He dragged them away from me!'

'Who did?' asked Pink-Whistle sharply.

'A bad boy,' wept the tiny girl. 'My mother will smack me for coming home without the sausages. It's that bad boy. He takes everything we have.'

Well, Pink-Whistle had to buy a string of sausages then. It was really quite an expensive morning for him. He didn't see the bad boy. He wondered where he was.

'Nobody really knows,' said the little girl, who was now all smiles again, trotting along by Pink-Whistle, holding tightly to his hand. 'You see, he hides — and pounces out. We never see him come. He runs so fast, too, no one can ever catch him.'

'I see,' said Pink-Whistle. 'Well, I shall look out for him!'

'You'll never see him,' said the tiny girl. 'He only pounces out on children smaller than himself. If you were a child, going shopping, you would see him soon enough!'

Pink-Whistle thought that was a good idea. Of course — he was sure to see that bad boy if he were a small child! It was only small children he robbed.

So, as soon as the small girl had run in at her gate, Pink-Whistle stepped into a lonely passage and muttered a few magic words. And no sooner were the words said than he had gone as small as a child of six!

He looked a bit queer because he still wore his own clothes. But that didn't bother Pink-Whistle.

He murmured a few more words and hey presto, he was dressed like a little boy, in jersey and grey shorts!

Pink-Whistle set out along the street, carrying a big teddy-bear, which had appeared at the same time as the jersey and shorts. He met one or two grown-ups who didn't take any notice of him at all.

He turned down another road where there was not a soul to be seen. He had gone about half-way when he came to an empty house and garden – and out of the gate darted a big boy, about fourteen, with a horrid, spiteful face.

'Stop,' said the big boy, and Pink-Whistle stopped. 'Give me that bear!' said the boy.

'No,' said Pink-Whistle. But the boy snatched the bear roughly from his hands and ran off with it.

He didn't run far, because something very queer happened. The bear bit him!

The bad boy felt the nip in his hand and looked down in astonishment. He thought something had stung him. The bear bit him again, and the boy cried out in alarm. He tried to drop the teddy bear, but the bear hung on to him for all it was worth, biting and nipping whenever it could find a bit of flesh.

'Oooh!' said the boy in great alarm. 'Are you alive? Stop it! That hurt!'

But the bear climbed all over him, biting and snapping, having a perfectly lovely time. Then

it slipped down the boy's leg and ran all the way back to Pink-Whistle. The little man whispered to it and it disappeared into thin air. So did Pink-Whistle.

He followed the bad boy, then slipped ahead of him, made himself visible and turned back to meet him again. There was no one else about at all.

As Pink-Whistle, who had now changed himself into a little girl, came near the bad boy, he jingled some money in his hand. The bad boy stopped at once.

'Give me that money!'

'No,' said Pink-Whistle, and pretended to cry in fright, like a little girl. The bad boy caught hold of his hand, forced it open roughly and took out the pennies Pink-Whistle was holding. He ran off with them.

Pink-Whistle stood and watched. Presently the bad boy stopped and looked down at the money in his hand. The pennies seemed to be awfully hot!

'Funny!' said the boy. 'They are almost burning my hand, they're so hot! Ow! I'll put them into my pockets!'

So he did — but they got hotter and hotter and hotter, and the boy could feel them burning a hole and hurting him! Then, to his horror, he saw smoke coming from his pockets! He turned them inside out and the pennies rolled away. But oh, what holes they had burnt!

The bad boy went on, puzzled. He didn't hear Pink-Whistle coming past him, invisible, his feet making no noise at all.

And when he met the little man again, he did not look like Mr Pink-Whistle, but like a sturdy little boy, carrying a small bag in which were some fine glass marbles.

The bad boy stopped and looked at the bag. 'What's in there?' he said roughly.

'My marbles,' said Pink-Whistle, in a little-boy voice.

'Let me see them,' said the bad boy.

'No,' said Pink-Whistle.

'You let me see them!' roared the bad boy, and Pink-Whistle meekly opened the bag. In a trice the big boy snatched it away, marbles and all, for he could see what fine ones they were.

Then off he ran. Pink-Whistle stood and watched him.

The bag felt very heavy after a bit. The boy looked down at it. It seemed bigger than he thought — almost a little sack. He decided to put it over his shoulder. It would be easier to carry that way.

So he put it over his left shoulder and set off again. But with every step he took the sack felt heavier and heavier and heavier. It weighed the boy down. He tried to take it off his shoulder, but he couldn't. He panted and puffed, and at last stopped, almost squashed to bits under the enormous weight.

Some children came running by and they stopped in surprise to see the bad boy weighed down by the enormous sack. They all knew him. He had taken things from each one of them at some time or other.

'What a horrid smell the sack has!' said one child. 'What's in it?'

'Help me to get it off my shoulder!' begged the bad boy. One of the children slit a hole in the sack — and out came a stream of rotten apples!

'Ho! He's carrying rotten apples!' cried the child. 'Where did you steal those?'

'They're marbles, not apples!' said the bad boy, in surprise. But they weren't. He was carrying nothing but hundreds of rotten apples! How extraordinary!

And then the children had a lovely time. They pulled the sack away from the bad boy, spilt all the rotten apples, and pelted him with them as hard as they could. Pink-Whistle joined in, you may be sure. A good punishment was just what the bad boy needed!

He ran off at last, crying bitterly, for he was not at all brave. Pink-Whistle, now looking like a little girl, met him as he went down the road. Pink-Whistle carried a handbag, and felt certain that the boy would stop.

But he didn't. He had had enough of taking things away from children. There was something queer about that day. So Pink-Whistle, looking just like a nice little girl, stopped the boy instead.

'I've got a whole shilling in my bag!' said Pink-Whistle, shaking it so that the money jingled.

'Keep it!' said the bad boy, wiping his dirty, tear-stained face.

'There's nobody about. You can easily take it away from me!' said Pink-Whistle.

'I'm never going to take anything from

anyone again,' said the boy. 'Never!'

Pink-Whistle suddenly changed into himself again, and to the boy's enormous surprise the little girl was no longer there — but a solemn-faced little man stood in front of him.

'Do you mean that?' asked Pink-Whistle, sternly. 'Or do you want a few more lessons?'

'Oh, no, no!' cried the boy. 'I'd be afraid of stopping anyone now. You've no idea the awful things that have happened to me today!'

'Serves you right,' said Pink-Whistle. 'Now you listen to me. You be kind in future to all those children you've stolen from, and give them pennies and sweets whenever you can. That will show me you're sorry. See? Else maybe awful things will happen to you again!'

'I will, I will,' promised the bad boy, and ran home, frightened and worried. He thought about it the whole afternoon, and decided that he had better keep his word.

So, to the great astonishment of all the small children round about, the bad boy stopped them and gave them things, instead of taking things away from them. And soon they were very fond of him, and ran to meet him whenever they saw him.

'I wish I could meet that funny little fellow again and tell him how much happier I am now,' the bad boy thought to himself a great many times. 'He might like me. I wish I could meet him.'

But Pink-Whistle was far away by that time, putting something else right. I do hope he comes along if anything goes wrong for you!

8

Mr Pink-Whistle and the money-box

For some time Mr Pink-Whistle hadn't come across anything to put right, and he was feeling very pleased about it.

'Perhaps the world is getting a better place,' he thought to himself. 'Perhaps people are being nicer to one another, and kinder. Maybe I needn't go around any more looking for things to put right. Perhaps I can go back to my own little cottage and live there peacefully with Sooty, my cat.'

But that very day Pink-Whistle had to change his mind, because he found two very unhappy children.

Pink-Whistle was walking in the lane that ran at the back of their garden, and he heard one of the children crying.

'Never mind,' said a boy's voice. 'Never mind, Katie. We shall have to save up again, that's all.'

'But it was such a mean thing to do to us,' sobbed Katie. 'That's what's making me cry. It was such a horrid, mean, unkind thing.'

Pink-Whistle peeped over the wall. He saw two children near by – a boy and a girl. They both looked very upset, but the boy wasn't crying.

'What's the matter?' asked Pink-Whistle. 'Can I do anything to help?'

'No, I'm afraid not,' said the boy. 'You see, it's like this. Katie and I have been saving up for our mother's birthday – we know exactly what she wants – that big red shawl in the draper's. It's a lovely one.'

'I know. I've seen it,' said Pink-Whistle.

'Well, it costs a lot of money,' said the boy. 'But Katie and I have been doing all kinds of jobs to earn the money for it.'

'We ran errands and we delivered papers,' said Katie, rubbing her eyes.

'I helped the farmer to lift his potatoes,' said the boy. 'And that's hard work.'

'And I took Mrs Brown's baby out each day for a week when she was ill,' said Katie. 'She gave me sixpence for that.'

'And I weeded old Mr Kent's garden, and he gave me a shilling,' said the boy. 'We put it all into our money-box pig.'

'Oh, was your money-box in the shape of a pig?' asked Mr Pink-Whistle. 'I like that sort of money-box.'

'It was a tin pig, painted pink, and it had a slit in its back,' said Katie. 'And it had a little key hanging on its tail to unlock a sort of little door in its tummy. We got the money out of the little door when we wanted it.'

'The pig was so nice and full,' said the boy. 'It jingled when we shook it. We were sure we had nearly enough to buy the shawl, and it is Mother's birthday next week. But now all our money is gone!'

'Where's it gone?' said Pink-Whistle, surprised.

'Someone stole it,' said Katie, her eyes filling with tears again. 'We took it out here in the garden, meaning to count out the money. Then Mother called us in for our biscuits and we ran indoors, and when we came out the pig was gone, and all the money with it.'

'Somebody must have come by, looked over the wall, and seen the money-box pig,' said the boy, sadly. 'Now all our hard work is wasted — and we shall never get enough money to buy that shawl.'

'It really is a shame,' said Mr Pink-Whistle, getting quite red with anger. 'It's not fair that someone should come along and take all the money you've worked hard to get. Perhaps I have got some for you. Wait a minute. Let me look in my pockets.'

But Pink-Whistle had only two pennies that day, so that wasn't much use. He rubbed one of his pointed ears and frowned. What could he do? He must do something!

Someone called the children. 'We must go,' said Katie. 'It's time for our dinner. Thank you for being so nice.'

The children ran off. Mr Pink-Whistle went on down the lane, remembering the girl's tear-stained face and the boy's look of disappointment. What a shame to steal from children!

'Well, I shall do something!' said Pink-Whistle, fiercely. 'But I don't know what. It seems to me as if all I can do is to poke my nose

86

into every house I see, and try to find that money-box pig!'

So he made himself invisible, and began to peep into the windows of all the houses he passed. But he didn't see any money-box pig at all.

He went on and on, peering into kitchens and sitting-rooms, trying to discover a money-box pig – and at last he found one!

It was standing on the mantelpiece of a neat little cottage, next to a ticking clock. There was a man in the room, reading. He looked smart and clean and neat – but Pink-Whistle didn't really like his face.

'Too clever!' thought Pink-Whistle. 'Too sharp! He looks as if he would do people a bad turn if he could, and think himself clever to do it! And there's the money-box pig, standing on the mantelpiece. Can it be the pig the children had stolen from them? Surely this well-dressed man here wouldn't steal such a thing as a child's money-box. He looks quite well-off.'

Someone went up the path and knocked at the door. The man inside looked up, got up quickly, took the money-box pig and put it under a cushion. Then Pink-Whistle knew he had stolen it. 'Aha!' said the little man to himself, 'aha! He wouldn't hide it if he hadn't stolen it. The mean fellow!'

The man opened the door to his friend, and Pink-Whistle slipped in beside him. He was quite invisible, so no one knew he was there.

'You're early,' said the first man. 'The others haven't arrived yet.'

'Oho!' thought Pink-Whistle, 'so there is to be a meeting. I think I'll stay – and have a bit of fun!'

So he stood in a corner, and then, when he had a chance to do it, he slipped his hand under the cushion and took out the pig. He stood it on the mantelpiece.

He shook it and the money jingled. Then Pink-Whistle made a grunting noise, just like a little pig, and spoke in a funny, piggy voice. 'Take me back, take me back!'

Mr Crooky, the man who lived in the cottage, looked up, very startled, and so did his friend. It seemed to them as if the money-box pig on the mantelpiece was jigging up and down and talking. They couldn't see Pink-Whistle moving it, of course.

'How extraordinary!' said the friend. Mr Crooky got up and took hold of the pig very roughly. He took it into the kitchen and put it on the dresser there. He slammed the door and came back. There was a knock at the front door and two more men came into the meeting.

Pink-Whistle grinned. He slipped quietly into the kitchen, found the pig, came back, shut the kitchen door softly, and, when no one was looking, placed the pig on the mantelpiece again!

Then he jiggled it hard and grunted in a piggy way again, talking in a funny, squeaky voice. 'Take me back! Take me back! I don't belong to you. Take me back!'

All the four men stopped talking and stared in astonishment at the jigging pig. Mr Crooky

went very red and looked most alarmed. How
had that pig got down from the dresser, opened
the kitchen door, and got back to the mantelpiece? How was it that it grunted and jigged
and talked like that? It must be magic!

'What does it mean, saying that it wants to
be taken back?' asked one of the men. 'Doesn't
it belong to you?'

'Of course it does,' said Mr Crooky. 'I can't
imagine what's come over the pig. I never
knew a tin pig behave like that before.'

'Oh, you bad story-teller, oh you wicked
man!' squeaked Pink-Whistle, making the pig
dance all round the mantelpiece as if it was
angry. 'You stole me! You know you did! Take
me back, take me back!'

'This is very strange,' said one of the men
looking hard at Crooky. 'What does it mean?'

'Nothing. It's just a silly joke of some sort,'

said Mr Crooky, beginning to tremble. 'I'll throw the pig into the dustbin.'

So he snatched it up, went into the yard and threw the pig hard into the dustbin. He slammed on the lid and went back to the house. How tiresome of this to happen just when he had called a meeting to ask his friends to give him money to start a shop! Now they might not trust him!

Pink-Whistle had gone into the yard with Mr Crooky. As soon as Crooky had gone back, Pink-Whistle took off the lid and fished out the pig. It was covered with tea-leaves.

Pink-Whistle crept to the window. It was open. To the men's enormous surprise, the money-box pig suddenly appeared on the window-sill, jigging and capering like mad, and a grunting voice could be heard at the same time. Then came the squeaky piggy voice.

'You bad man! You put me in the dustbin! I'm covered with tea-leaves – but you ought to be covered with shame! You stole me from those children. You know you did. Take me back, take me back!'

'This is most extraordinary and most disgraceful,' said one of the men, standing up. 'Mr Crooky, take that pig back at once. If you don't, I shall call the village policeman and ask him to listen to all the pig says.'

Mr Crooky felt as if he were in a bad dream. He stared at the pig, which turned a somersault and rattled like mad. 'I'm hungry!' it squeaked, 'I'm hungry. You put something into me, quick! I'm hungreeeeeeeeeeeh!'

Mr Crooky felt so frightened that he put his hand into his pocket and pulled out all the money there. He popped it into the slit in the pig's back.

'More, more!' cried the pig, and Mr Crooky put in more and more till he had no money left. 'Now take me home, home, home!' cried the pig, and leapt high into the air and back again to the window-sill. Mr Crooky thought that either he or the pig must be mad, or perhaps both of them. Or maybe it was a frightening kind of dream.

'Well, I'd better take you back, and then perhaps I shall wake up,' he said. So he snatched up the dancing pig, and ran off with it at top speed. He came to the children's garden and threw the pig over the wall. It landed on the grass.

Mr Crooky turned to go home. 'Now don't you *ever* do such a wicked thing again!' a voice boomed in his ear, making him almost jump out of his skin. It was Mr Pink-Whistle, of course, having one last smack at Mr Crooky. The man tore off down the lane as if a hundred dogs were after him. Mr Pink-Whistle made himself visible and climbed over the wall into the garden. He called the children.

They came running to him and he showed them the pig, which he had picked up. 'Here you are,' he said. 'Safely back again – and heavier than before.'

The children shouted with delight. They undid the little door in the pig's tummy and the money tumbled out. What a lot there was now!

'More than we ever put in!' cried Katie. 'Oh, how marvellous! How did it happen, little man? Tell us, do!'

But Pink-Whistle had vanished again. He didn't like being thanked. It was enough to see the children's joyful faces, and to know that they could buy their mother the present they had saved up for – and could buy her something else besides now!

As for Mr Crooky, he didn't get the money lent to him for the shop he wanted to start – and a very good thing, too! He is still puzzled whenever he thinks of that grunting, dancing, talking pig, but if he happens to read this story, he won't be puzzled any more!

9

Mr Pink-Whistle has a good idea

One day Mr Pink-Whistle was going along
down a quiet road, when he saw a face looking
at him out of a window.

It was a nice face. It belonged to an old lady,
whose hair shone silvery-grey in the sunshine,
and whose eyes were blue and kind. But it was
a sad face.

'I'll go by here tomorrow, and see if the old
lady is still looking out,' thought Pink-Whistle.
'I shall be seeing that poor old pony in the field
at the bottom of this road every day for some
time, so I can easily come down this road and
look out for the old lady.'

Mr Pink-Whistle had made a new friend – a
very old pony, who had worked hard all his life
long, pulling heavy carts and taking his master
to market.

He would have been very happy if he had
had a kind master, but the man he worked for
was rough and impatient, too ready with the
whip, and always shouting.

And now, when the pony was too old to pull
heavy carts any more, and had been shut into
the field, he was lonely and afraid.

'You see,' he said to Pink-Whistle, who,

being half a brownie, understood animals very
well, 'you see, Mr Pink-Whistle, I'm afraid that
my master, now that I am no good to him, may
sell me off to someone who will work me to
death, and I really feel very tired and old now. I
could do a little light work, but I'm afraid I
couldn't do heavy work any more. I should fall
down, and then I should be lashed and shouted
at.'

'It's a shame,' said Pink-Whistle. 'It really is.
But perhaps your master won't sell you to
anyone who will work you like that. He
certainly is not a kind or just man, but I don't
believe his wife would let him do anything
horrid to you.'

'He might even sell me to be killed and sold
as horseflesh,' said the poor old pony. 'You
see, I really am no use to him now! I might pull
a baby's pram, but I couldn't pull a cart any

more. Oh, Mr Pink-Whistle, I do feel so lonely and afraid sometimes. I don't know what I should do if you didn't come and talk to me.'

'Now I really can't bear this,' thought kind Pink-Whistle to himself, each time he left the old pony. 'What am I to do? I must put this right somehow, but how? Nobody wants a pony like that, and yet he deserves a little kindness and friendliness now, after having worked so hard and well all his life. It isn't fair.'

It wasn't fair. The farmer should have gone sometimes to the field, patted the old pony, and cheered him up. He should have told him that he could live out the rest of his days in peace and sunshine. But he didn't. He just grumbled because he couldn't get any more work out of him.

'If I could hear of anyone that wants an old pony like that I'd sell him,' he said to his wife. 'He's perfectly useless to me, but anyone with an old cab could still get a bit of work out of him.'

'Well, it's a good thing that there are so few horse-cabs now,' said his wife. 'I'd hate you to sell old Brownie to a cab-man, who might whip him and try to make his poor old legs go faster than they can.'

Pink-Whistle thought a lot about the old pony. Anyone or anything in trouble made his kind heart very heavy and sad. And now he began to worry about the old lady who looked out of the window he passed every day.

'She looks so sad and lonely. She's got the same look in her eyes as the old pony. When people get old and tired they shouldn't be allowed to be sad and lonely.'

Every day he looked at the old lady and soon he began to smile and wave as he passed. She smiled back and waved, too. Each time Pink-Whistle went to see the old pony he kept a special smile for the old lady in the window.

Then one day he found some marigolds growing wild on a rubbish-heap at the bottom of the field where the old pony lived. 'I'll take those to the old lady!' thought Pink-Whistle. So he picked them, made them into a nice little bunch, and that day, instead of passing the gate where the old lady lived, he opened it and marched up to the door!

But nobody opened it. A voice from the window said: 'I'm so sorry I can't open the door. I can't walk without help. Will you come to the window?'

So Pink-Whistle went to the window,

beamed at the old lady, and gave her the marigolds. She put them into a glass of water and beamed back.

'How kind you are!' she said. 'I always look for your smile as you go down the street. Where do you go?'

Pink-Whistle told her about the old pony. The old woman listened with great interest.

'Poor old thing,' she said. 'Once I used to be rich and I had a pony-cart and pony of my own, and I used to drive about. Now I am poor, and somehow I have no friends. I am a poor, helpless old woman, no use to anyone — just like the old pony!'

'Can't you walk?' asked Pink-Whistle. 'If you could get about a bit you could soon make friends!'

'No, I can't walk,' said the old lady. 'There is something wrong with my legs. I did have a good friend who came in every day to take me out in my bath-chair — but now she has moved far away, and the woman who said she would come is cross and busy — too busy to take me out at all. She cleans my room for me, and helps me in and out of bed — but she can't spare the time to take me out.'

'So you never go out?' said Pink-Whistle. 'Well, well — what a pity! You must be very lonely and dull. I must come and see you sometimes.'

So he went to see her, and one day he pulled out the bath-chair from the cupboard it had stood in for months and managed to get the old lady tucked up in it. Then out they went — and the first thing Pink-Whistle did was to take her to see the old pony!

Well, you can guess how the two old things liked one another! The old lady had always loved horses — and the pony was delighted to find someone who knew how to talk to him, and click to him, and offer him a carrot. He nuzzled his brown head into her shoulder, and it was all Pink-Whistle could do to make them part.

One day the old lady was very excited. She had had a letter from her friend — and in it was some money!

'Look!' she said to Pink-Whistle. 'Money! But I don't want money at my age. So I am going to give it all to you, dear Mr Pink-Whistle, every bit — and you must buy a present for yourself from a grateful old lady. I don't know what I should have done without you.'

'I don't want your money,' said Pink-Whistle, smiling. 'You keep it and buy yourself a new shawl and a new armchair.'

The old lady's eyes filled with tears. 'I don't want anything for myself,' she said. 'I did so want you to have the money, Mr Pink-Whistle. There is nothing I can do for you, nothing at all, in return for the happiness you have given to me — and I did think, I really did think this would be a little return for all your kindness.'

Pink-Whistle didn't know what to do. He felt as if he couldn't take money from the old lady — and yet she would be terribly unhappy if he didn't. After all, it *is* lovely to pay back

kindness – and there was no other way she
could do it.

And then a grand idea came into Pink-
Whistle's head, and he grinned his wide grin.
He held out his hand. 'I'll take the money,' he
said, 'but on one condition, old friend – that I
can do exactly as I like with it!'

'Of course you can,' said the old lady gladly, and gave him the money. Pink-Whistle trotted off quickly, full of his idea.

He went to the farmer who lived in his farmhouse beside the pony's field. He asked him how much the old pony was.

There was enough money to buy him. 'May I keep him in the field when he is not in use?' asked Pink-Whistle. The farmer said yes. Pink-Whistle trotted back to the old lady's house. He pulled out her bath-chair, and went off with it. She didn't see him, because she was asleep.

The little man took the chair to a leather-worker and asked him to fit it up so that it could be drawn along by a pony. 'That's easy,' said the man. 'You'll want reins, of course – and little shafts put here – and this bit altered there. I can do it in two days.'

'I'll help you, Dad,' said the man's small boy, a smiling, merry-eyed lad. ' 'Tisn't often we do a job like this, is it? I'd like to see a pony drawing this bath-chair. Is there a pony for it, Mister?'

'Yes,' said Pink-Whistle, and told the boy all about it. Then a good idea came to him. 'I suppose you wouldn't like to fetch the pony from the field every day to the old lady's house, and harness him to the bath-chair for her, would you?' he said. 'You're not very big and you could ride on the pony's back to and from the field.'

'Ooooooh, yes,' said the small boy, his eyes shining with delight. 'I love horses. I'd just love that. Dad, may I do that?'

Pink-Whistle left the workshop, feeling very pleased. He had spent the old lady's money well! He had done something that would make the old pony very happy, for now he would have a friend, a nice light job of work — and a little boy to talk to him and even ride on his back a little each day. And the small boy would have some fun and feel quite important riding the pony, and harnessing him to the bath-chair each day.

'Well, it's wonderful what can be done if you really think hard enough,' said Pink-Whistle, trotting down the road very happily. 'I do wonder what the old lady will say!'

Well, you should have seen her face the first day that the little boy came into the garden riding the old pony! Pink-Whistle arrived too, with the altered bath-chair. The little boy

jumped down, and fitted straps and reins as his father had shown him. They both smiled and waved at the astonished old lady.

Then Pink-Whistle went into the house and helped the old lady to hobble slowly along to the bath-chair. She couldn't walk properly, she could only hobble a few steps. She got into the chair and Pink-Whistle tucked her up. He gave her the reins.

'Now, you said you know how to drive a horse,' he said. 'You needn't be afraid that the pony will go fast, because he won't. He's too old. He's so pleased to come and do a job of work like this for you. He's yours. I bought him with your money. Now – off you go!'

And off they went, the old lady driving the pony, and steering the bath-chair at the same time in a very clever way – but as the pony only walked slowly, there wasn't any danger of the old lady having an accident at all.

'Well, that's a fine sight to see, isn't it?' said Pink-Whistle, pleased, as he stared down the road after the two old friends, his hand on the small boy's shoulder. 'Now, you look out for them to come back – and take out the pony and ride him back to the field. Look after the old lady, too, and help her into the house.'

Good old Pink-Whistle! The old lady is as happy as she can be, driving out with her pony every day – and the old pony isn't afraid or lonely any more, because she is his friend. And he has the little boy, too, to talk to him and ride him carefully, and bring him a lump of sugar for a treat.

But the happiest of them all is Pink-Whistle, of course. 'There's nothing like putting bad things right,' he says. 'It's the finest thing anyone can do.'

I think so, too, don't you?

10

Mr Pink-Whistle and the eggs

Annabelle had five hens. Grandpa had given them to her on her last birthday, when they were quite small. Now they were big, and just beginning to lay.

Annabelle was delighted. 'Mummy, you shall have an egg for your breakfast every day!' she said. 'And so shall Daddy. And I will take two round to Granny and Grandpa every day, and there will be one egg for my breakfast, too. You will lay me five eggs, won't you, little red hens?'

The five hens looked at Annabelle and clucked. They liked this little girl who fed them each day, gave them fresh water, and cleaned out their house three times a week. They liked the way she talked to them, too. So they all clucked back, and Annabelle knew quite well what they said.

'They say they will certainly lay me five eggs every day,' she told her mother.

They did. Each morning when little Annabelle went to look in the nesting-boxes there were five smooth brown eggs. Not very big ones, because the hens were young, but, oh, how delicious they tasted!

Daddy and Mummy had one each day. So did Annabelle. She took two round to Granny and Grandpa, always the biggest two, because it was Grandpa who had given her the little red hens.

And then one morning when Annabelle went to look for the eggs there was not a single one! All the nesting-boxes were empty. What a shock for Annabelle. She stared at the empty boxes and then at the hens.

'Why haven't you laid me any eggs?' she said.

The hens clucked loudly. 'Cuck-cuck-cuck, we did, we did!' they said.

'You didn't,' said Annabelle. 'There aren't any at all. Please lay me some tomorrow.'

But there weren't any the next day either. Annabelle couldn't understand it. 'Perhaps

someone is taking them,' she thought. 'Oh, dear, what a horrid thing to do.'

The next day there were no eggs again. Annabelle cried bitterly. 'It's a shame!' she said to the hens. 'I am sure somebody is stealing your eggs. It's a shame! You are my own hens, and you lay beautiful eggs that are mine – and now somebody else is taking them.'

A big black cat with green eyes was wandering by, not far from the hen-house. It stopped when it heard Annabelle crying, and listened to what she said.

Then it ran off quickly to its master. The cat was Sooty, Mr Pink-Whistle's own cat. It mewed for its master, and Mr Pink-Whistle came hurrying from the kitchen, where he was busy cleaning out his larder.

'A job for you to do, Master!' mewed Sooty. 'You leave the larder to me. I'll clean it all right! I've found a better job for you to do than that.'

'What is it?' asked Mr Pink-Whistle. 'Is it something I can put right? I haven't done a job like that for some time.'

'Yes, you can put it right, I expect,' said Sooty, and told Mr Pink-Whistle what had happened to Annabelle. 'She's such a dear little girl,' said Sooty. 'And somebody is really being very unkind, Master, to steal all her eggs.'

'I'll soon put that right!' said Mr Pink-Whistle, briskly. 'Where does she live? Oh, not very far away. That's good.'

Now, the next morning, just as it was

106

beginning to get light, Mr Pink-Whistle went out. He made his way to Annabelle's house. Just as he turned in at her front gate he made himself invisible. Hey, presto! One moment he was there, and the next he was not. At least, he was, but nobody could see him.

He went down the garden to the hen-house. Scamp, the dog, heard him and smelt him, but couldn't see him. He growled a little in fright but didn't bark.

Mr Pink-Whistle went right to the bottom of the garden, where a tall hedge stood. Just beside it was the hen-house. Mr Pink-Whistle had a look round. Nobody about just yet. He opened the hen-house door and felt in the nesting-boxes. Four eggs already – and a hen sitting in the fifth box!

He went out and shut the door softly. Then he stood on the path and waited in the dim light. He felt certain that the thief would soon be coming along, whoever he was.

Then very softly and silently, so that even Scamp's sharp ears heard no sound, somebody came through a gap in the hedge. Pink-Whistle looked at him. Dear, dear – who ever would have thought him to be the thief?

'It's Mr Smarmy,' said Pink-Whistle to himself. 'He goes to church. He sings hymns very loudly indeed. He always shakes his head and looks shocked when he hears of someone who has done wrong. And all the time he is taking little Annabelle's eggs!'

Mr Smarmy was well-dressed and neat. Even coming through the hedge had not made him untidy. He tiptoed to the hen-house, opened the door, and felt about for eggs. One, two, three, four, five. Good! He put them carefully into his five pockets, and then went out. He backed through the hedge and pulled the branches together behind him. He was gone.

'So it's Mr Smarmy,' said Pink-Whistle again. 'I never did like him. Always so down on other people. Always finding fault with his gentle little wife. Always pretending to be so good and proper. Dear, dear — what a very horrid fellow, to be sure. I never did like deceitful people. Now what's to be done?'

Pink-Whistle went off to his own home. He went to his larder and looked in the egg-rack. There were six eggs there. He took five of

them. He went back to the hen-house and popped them into the nesting boxes. 'Now Annabelle won't be disappointed!' he said. 'And tomorrow I'll play a nice little trick on Mr Smarmy.'

The eggs were white ones, not brown. Annabelle was most astonished when she found them that morning. 'Look, Mummy!' she said. 'There are eggs this morning all right – but they are white, not brown. Isn't that queer?'

Now, that day Mr Pink-Whistle spent in a very queer way. He made five magic eggs, and how he chuckled as he made them. Sooty watched him and chuckled too.

Early the next morning Mr Pink-Whistle went along to Annabelle's hen-house again. There were five brown eggs there. He put them carefully into his pocket, and then put five magic eggs into the nesting-boxes instead. Then, quite invisible, he waited for Mr Smarmy to come along. The thief came silently through the hedge. He went into the hen-house and put the eggs carefully into his five pockets. Then he went out again.

Mr Pink-Whistle chuckled once more. He waited till Mr Smarmy had gone, then he popped back into the hen-house and put the brown eggs from his pocket into the nesting-boxes. Annabelle would find them there, quite safely.

Then he went home to breakfast. Sooty had got it ready for him. The big black cat laughed when he heard what his master had done.

'One of the magic eggs will go POP very loudly indeed,' said Mr Pink-Whistle. 'One will burst and make a very horrible smell. One will mew like a cat. One will cluck like a hen, and the last one will grow tiny legs and run all over Mr Smarmy.'

Sooty giggled, and when a cat giggles it

sounds very funny indeed. 'I wish I was going to see all that,' said Sooty.

'Well, I'm going to!' said Mr Pink-Whistle. 'I want to see Mr Smarmy taught a lesson. It's quite time he was!'

Now, Mr Smarmy, after he had taken the eggs, went to his sister Lucy's for breakfast. He didn't give her any of the eggs. Oh, no! He was going to take those home, after he had done his work that day, and ask his wife to make a nice fat omelette for him.

'I've got a busy day, Lucy,' he said. 'Got to see a lot of important people. Mustn't be late at the office. The first meeting is at half-past nine.'

Mr Smarmy arrived there at just before half-past nine. But he couldn't take any of the eggs out of his pockets because two of the men he was going to meet had already arrived.

'Good morning!' said Mr Smarmy. 'Nice and early! Aha! Here are the others, too!'

Soon seven men were sitting down round the table – and an eighth, who could not be seen, was standing opposite Mr Smarmy. That was Mr Pink-Whistle, of course, who had made himself invisible, and was at the meeting unknown to anyone.

The meeting began. Mr Smarmy wanted to ask the six men round him to lend him money for his business, so he was very polite indeed. Everyone listened to him quietly – till the first-egg went POP.

'POP!' It burst with a loud noise, rather like a paper bag when it is blown up and goes bang. Everyone jumped and looked at Mr Smarmy.

He looked alarmed. 'What was that?' he said.

'It sounded as if it came from somewhere about you,' said one man. 'Good gracious, look! What's that mess trickling out of one of your pockets? Looks like egg!'

It *was* egg, of course. Mr Smarmy looked down in disgust at the yellow mess that was seeping out of his pocket. How horrible! That egg must have been bad, to blow up like that!

He tried to wipe the mess away with his clean handkerchief. Then another egg began its magic work. It mewed like a cat!

'Mew-ew-ew-ew! Mew-ew-ew-ew!'

'There's a cat somewhere,' said one of the men. 'Sounds as if you've got it on your knee, Mr Smarmy.'

'Mew-ew-ew-ew!' Mr Smarmy jumped up in alarm, for the noise came from somewhere about him, there was no doubt of that. And then the mewing egg went off with a pop just as the other one had done!

Everyone jumped at the POP, and stared at another yellow mess coming from a pocket the other side of Mr Smarmy's coat. 'Is this some kind of a joke?' asked a man.

'No – no! I assure you I can't imagine *what* is happening!' said poor Mr Smarmy. 'Oh, dear – there goes another one!'

'POP!' Another egg burst, and this time there was such a terrible smell that everyone got out their handkerchiefs at once. 'Pooh,' said one of the men. 'Smarmy, do you often carry bad eggs about? I hope you are not a bad egg yourself! Pooh! What a fearful smell.'

112

Mr Smarmy was most distressed. This meeting was not going at all well. Blow those eggs! He wished he hadn't taken them that morning. They must all be bad ones. He heard a little chuckle close to his ear and turned in alarm.

It was Mr Pink-Whistle, but, of course, Mr

Smarmy couldn't see him. Pink-Whistle was having a lovely time. What a joke! It was nice to see a horrid person like Mr Smarmy getting into trouble like this.

The meeting went on again after Mr Smarmy had tried to clean himself up. And then the fourth egg began to cluck like a hen. It went off very loudly indeed.

'Cuck-cuck-cuck-cuck-cuck! Cuck-cuck-cuck-cuck-cuck! CUCK-CUCK!'

'Good gracious! He's got a hen in his pocket now!' cried one of the men. 'Smarmy, what is the meaning of this? Is this the way to get us to lend money to you – to play idiotic tricks of this kind?'

'Sir, I assure you –' began poor Mr Smarmy, clutching in alarm at the egg that was clucking, but before he could finish it went POP, too! And then there was another yellow mess to clear up!

'Do you always carry bad eggs about with you?' asked one of the men. 'Have you any more? If so, I advise you to remove them from your pockets, Smarmy. We've had enough of eggs this morning.'

'There's one more,' said poor Smarmy, putting his hand into a pocket. 'I'll take it out. Oh – it's running away from me! Oh, it's gone down my trouser leg! Now it's running up again! It's inside my vest. It's tickling me. It's got legs, I'm sure!'

All the men stared at Mr Smarmy in amazement. The egg had grown legs, just as Pink-Whistle had said it would, and was running about all over him. He kept clutching

114

at it, but it always slipped away somewhere else.

'He's mad!' said one of the men, getting up. 'Well, I didn't come here to have egg-tricks played on me. I'm not putting any money into a business run by a man who plays silly conjuring tricks with eggs that pop and mew and cluck and grow legs. Not I!'

'Nor I!' cried all the others, and they got up to go. Mr Smarmy stared at them in dismay. 'Please, please wait!' he cried. 'This is the last egg. Do wait!'

POP! The last egg burst, too – and that was enough for the men. They went out of the room, talking loudly about people who seemed to think it was funny to play tricks with bad eggs. Mr Smarmy was left alone, with a burst egg trickling down his leg.

He groaned. Then he felt a tap on his shoulder. He looked up in surprise, to see Mr Pink-Whistle looking sternly down at him. It made Mr Smarmy jump to see him there so suddenly.

'This is what happens to people who steal eggs from a little girl's hens,' said Mr Pink-Whistle. 'Bad things always come from bad deeds. None of those men will lend you the money you want. It serves you right.'

Mr Smarmy groaned again and buried his face in his hands. 'It does, I know it does,' he said. 'I'm a deceitful fellow. I pretend to be so good – and yet I am mean enough to take eggs belonging to a little girl's hens. I deserve all this. I don't know who you are, or how you know about it, or why those eggs behaved like

that – I only know I'm ashamed and sorry.'

'That's good,' said Mr Pink-Whistle, pleased. 'Very good. What about buying a beautiful doll for the little girl, and putting it in the hen-house for her to find tomorrow, to make up for the eggs you took, Mr Smarmy? And what about trying to be as good and proper as you are always pretending to be? If you are really sorry, you can do that, too.'

And then away went Mr Pink-Whistle to tell Sooty all that had happened. But you may be sure he will be hiding, unseen, in the hen-house on the morning when there is a beautiful new doll waiting for Annabelle. She will be so surprised and pleased – and dear old Pink-Whistle wants to see her happy face.

He really is a kind old thing, isn't he?

11

Mr Pink-Whistle goes to school

Mr Pink-Whistle was walking down the road
wondering if the fishmonger had any kippers
for himself and Sooty, his cat, when four girls
and two boys came running along.

'Quick!' said one. 'Get round the corner
before Harry and George see us!'

They shot round the corner – and then came
the sound of pattering footsteps behind Mr
Pink-Whistle once more, and along came two
big boys, almost knocking him over.

Mr Pink-Whistle went spinning into the
gutter and just saved himself from sitting down
hard by clutching at a lamp-post.

The two boys didn't say they were sorry,
they didn't even stop! They rushed round the
corner after the smaller children.

'Good gracious!' said Mr Pink-Whistle,
letting go the lamp-post. 'What unpleasant
boys! Who are they, I wonder?'

He went round the corner. He saw Harry
and George pouncing on the smaller children
and taking their hats and caps away. They sent
them sailing up into the trees and over the
hedges!

'You are hateful,' said a small girl, beginning

117

to cry. 'You're always playing horrid tricks, and making us take the blame!'

'You hid my French book yesterday and I got into trouble for it,' said Joan.

'You spilt my ink-pot all over the floor, and I had to stay in,' said Peter. 'I know you did it! It's just the kind of thing you always do.'

'Yes — and then you leave us to bear the blame,' said Doris. 'And if we tell tales of you you smack our faces and tramp on our toes!'

Harry pounced on Doris and pulled her hair so hard that she squealed.

'Let go!' she said.

Mr Pink-Whistle made himself invisible. He crept up to Harry, caught hold of his hair and tugged hard.

'Oh!' said Harry, and swung round. George

was just near by. 'Did you pull my hair? What do you think you're doing?'

'I didn't touch you,' said George. 'Don't be silly!'

Then the two boys glared at one another and put up their fists to fight. The other children saw their chance and ran off at once. Let them fight! They wouldn't bother the others then!

Mr Pink-Whistle didn't like the two boys at all. He took a look at them. Their faces were hard. It wouldn't be any good talking to them, or pleading with them to be better. They would laugh.

'No – the only thing is to do the same things to them that they do to others,' decided Mr Pink-Whistle. 'I shall go to school with these children this afternoon. Ha – there'll be a bit of fun then! But not for George or Harry!'

He waited for the children that afternoon and then walked along beside them, unseen. He saw how they all ran away from George and Harry, and how frightened of the two big boys they were.

'A couple of bullies!' said Mr Pink-Whistle. 'Well, well – bullies are always cowards, so we'll just see what Harry and George do when unpleasant things begin to happen to them. They shall take the blame for things I do this afternoon, in return for making others take the blame for things that they so often have done.'

He went into the schoolroom with Harry and George and the rest of their class. He noticed where the two big boys sat and went

119

over to them. Nobody could see him. He was quite invisible, of course.

When George was bending down to pick up a dropped pencil Mr Pink-Whistle opened his desk lid and let it drop with a terrific BANG!

Everyone jumped. The teacher frowned. 'George! There's no need to make that noise.'

'I didn't,' said George indignantly. 'I was bending down. Someone else must have banged my desk-lid.'

'Was it you, Harry?' asked the teacher. Harry always sat next to George.

'No, it wasn't,' said Harry, rudely.

Well, Mr Pink-Whistle managed to bang George's desk-lid twice more, and the teacher began to blame Harry, because George was so very indignant that she felt sure it couldn't be his fault.

The two boys glared at one another. Then Mr Pink-Whistle tipped a pile of books off Harry's desk when he wasn't looking!

'HARRY!' said the teacher.

'I didn't do it,' said Harry, angrily. 'Make George pick up my books. He must have done that.'

'I didn't,' said George. 'Yah!'

'Boys, boys!' said the teacher. 'George, come up here and write on the board for me. Write down the homework notes for tomorrow.'

George went up sulkily. He took up the chalk and began to write on the board. Mr Pink-Whistle was just behind him, invisible.

He took George's hand and began to guide

120

the piece of chalk. And do you know what he wrote? He wrote this: 'Harry is a silly donkey. Harry is a dunce. Harry is . . . .'

George was horrified. Whatever was the chalk doing? It seemed to be writing by itself, and he couldn't stop it. And look what it was writing too! Whatever would his teacher say? Where was the duster? He must rub out the rude writing at once!

Aha! Mr Pink-Whistle had taken the duster, of course. He had thrown it up to the top of a picture. George couldn't see it anywhere.

The children saw what George had written, and they began to nudge one another and giggle. The teacher turned to see what George was doing behind her – and dear me, she saw what he had written on the blackboard!

'GEORGE!' she said angrily. 'How dare you do that? What in the world are you thinking of? Rub it out at once.'

'I didn't mean to,' said poor George. 'It felt as if the chalk was writing by itself.'

'Oh, don't be so silly,' said the teacher. 'My goodness me — look where the duster has been thrown to! Did you throw it there, George? You'd better lose ten marks straight away for your silly behaviour this afternoon!'

Harry laughed like anything. He was angry with George for writing rude things about him on the board. Mr Pink-Whistle waited till George was back in his seat and then he pulled Harry's hair quite hard.

Harry jumped and glared round at George. Mr Pink-Whistle tugged at George's hair then. George jumped and glared round at Harry.

'Stop that!' they said to each other, and the teacher banged on her desk for quiet.

Well, Mr Pink-Whistle quite enjoyed himself that afternoon and so did all the class, except Harry and George. Harry's ruler shot off his desk. George's pencil-box upset all over the floor. Harry's shoelaces came mysteriously undone three times. George's socks kept slipping down to his ankles, and his jersey buttons came undone at his neck. It was all very extraordinary.

They all went out to play for ten minutes. Mr Pink-Whistle went with them. He kicked Harry's ball into the next-door garden. He tripped George up twice and sent him rolling over and over. The two boys got very angry indeed, because they both felt certain it was the other one playing tricks.

122

After a few minutes Mr Pink-Whistle went indoors. He went to Harry's desk and put half his books into George's. He put George's pencils into Harry's box. That was the kind of thing the two boys were always doing to other people. Well, let them see if they liked it or not!

They didn't like it a bit. Harry wailed aloud when he found half his books gone, because the teacher was always very cross when anyone was careless with books. And George was furious to find his best pencils missing.

'Who's taken them? Wait till I find out!' he cried angrily. 'Teacher – all my best pencils have gone!'

They were found in Harry's box almost at once, and George almost flew at him in rage. He would have hit him then and there if the teacher hadn't suddenly discovered that Harry's books were in George's desk! She was really disgusted.

'I thought you two boys were friends. Look at this — your books in George's desk, Harry, and all George's pencils in your box. You ought to be ashamed of yourselves. Any more nonsense from either of you and you will stay in for half an hour.'

Well, there was quite a lot of nonsense of course — but it was from Mr Pink-Whistle, not from the boys! He upset George's paint-pot all over his painting — a thing that George himself did to somebody almost every painting lesson! And he smudged Harry's best writing when he wasn't looking. And that, too, was something that Harry was very fond of doing to the smaller children.

The teacher was cross. 'Stay in for half an hour, both of you,' she said. 'I don't care if you *are* going out to a party. You can be half an hour late.'

'But you *know* it's my cousin's birthday party,' said George, indignantly. 'I *can't* be late.'

'I know all about the party — and I'm afraid you *will* be late, both of you!' said the teacher, firmly. The two boys glared at one another. Each felt sure it was the other who had got him into all this trouble!

They had to stay in for half an hour and do most of their work again. Then they said a sulky good-bye and went out.

As soon as they got out in the road they

began to quarrel. 'I suppose you think you were very clever this afternoon!' said George, angrily. 'Well, take *that*!'

And he hit Harry hard on the back. Mr Pink-Whistle grinned. A fight? Well, he would join in as well. He would repay both George and Harry the smacks and slaps and biffs and thuds that they had many a time dealt out to the younger children.

So, quite invisible, he hopped in and out, dealing a slap here and a smack there, and making the boys yell in pain, and go for each other all the more.

Biff! That was George hitting Harry on the nose. It began to bleed.

Smack! That was Harry hitting George on his right eye. It began to go black at once.

Thud, bang, slap! That was Mr Pink-Whistle doing his share!

BIFF-BANG! That was both boys at once – and they fell over, crash, into a muddy puddle. They sat up, howling.

'Let's stop,' wept George. 'My eye hurts. And your nose is bleeding. We're terribly late for the party. We shall miss all the good things at tea.'

So sniffing and snuffling, muddy, wet and very much the worse for wear, the two boys arrived at their cousin's house. But when their aunt saw them, she was very cross indeed.

'George! Harry! How *can* you come to a party looking like that? Have you been fighting one another? You should be ashamed of yourselves. One with a black eye and one with a bleeding nose! And so dirty and untidy too. I won't let you in. You shan't come to the party!'

And she slammed the door in their faces. They went howling down the street, very sorry for themselves.

Mr Pink-Whistle began to think they might have learnt their lesson. He suddenly appeared beside them, a kind little man with pointed ears.

'Come and have tea with me,' he said. 'I live not far off with my cat Sooty.'

So they went with him, still sniffing. He made them wash and brush their hair. He stopped Harry's nose from bleeding, and he bathed George's eye. Then he sat them down to bread and butter and honey and a seed-cake.

'You're very kind,' said George, surprised.

'I'm not always,' said Mr Pink-Whistle, solemnly. 'Sometimes, when I see mean, unkind people I get that way myself – just to punish them, you know. I've had a good time this afternoon, punishing two nasty little boys. My word, they were horrid little things – always teasing the smaller ones and getting them into trouble.'

The two boys gazed at him, afraid.

'You've no idea of the things I did!' said Mr Pink-Whistle, passing them the seed-cake. 'My, the tricks I played in their class this afternoon – and what a time I had when those boys fought. I fought, too – biff, bang, thud!'

The boys looked at one another

uncomfortably. They both felt very scared.

'You know, I always think that if mean, unkind people get treated meanly and unkindly themselves sometimes, they learn how horrid it is,' said Mr Pink-Whistle. 'Of course — they sometimes need more than one lesson — perhaps two, or four, or even six!'

He looked hard at the two boys. They looked back. 'Sir,' said George, in a small voice. 'We shan't need more than that one lesson. I promise you that.'

'I promise you, too,' said Harry, in a whisper. 'It's — it's very kind of you, sir, to take us home and give us this tea — when you know we're mean.'

'Bless us all, you can come again as often as you like — so long as you don't need another lesson from me, but only a nice tea!' said kind Mr Pink-Whistle. 'Now do take another piece of cake each — just to show there's no ill-feeling between us!'

Well, they did, of course. And, so far as I know, Mr Pink-Whistle hasn't had to give them another lesson — yet! But he would, you know, if they broke their promise. He's kind — but he's fierce, too, when he's putting wrong things right!

ENID BLYTON

If you are an eager Beaver reader, perhaps you ought to try some of our exciting Enid Blyton titles. They are available in bookshops or they can be ordered directly from us. Just complete the form below, enclose the right amount of money and the books will be sent to you at home.

☐	THE CHILDREN OF CHERRY-TREE FARM	£1.99
☐	THE CHILDREN OF WILLOW FARM	£1.99
☐	NAUGHTY AMELIA JANE	£1.50
☐	AMELIA JANE AGAIN	£1.50
☐	THE BIRTHDAY KITTEN	£1.50
☐	THE VERY BIG SECRET	£1.50
☐	THE ADVENTUROUS FOUR	£1.50
☐	THE ADVENTUROUS FOUR AGAIN	£1.50
☐	THE NAUGHTIEST GIRL IS A MONITOR	£1.95
☐	THE NAUGHTIEST GIRL IN THE SCHOOL	£1.95
☐	THE ENCHANTED WOOD	£1.99
☐	THE WISHING-CHAIR AGAIN	£1.99
☐	HURRAH FOR THE CIRCUS	£1.75

If you would like to order books, please send this form, and the money due to:
ARROW BOOKS, BOOKSERVICE BY POST, PO BOX 29, DOUGLAS, ISLE OF MAN, BRITISH ISLES. Please enclose a cheque or postal order made out to Arrow Books Ltd for the amount due including 22p per book for postage and packing both for orders within the UK and for overseas orders.

NAME ....

ADDRESS ....

....

Please print clearly.

Whilst every effort is made to keep prices low it is sometimes necessary to increase cover prices at short notice. Arrow Books reserve the right to show new retail prices on covers which may differ from those previously advertised in the text or elsewhere.